力得文化
Leader Culture

開啟生活的
字彙
聯想力

力得編輯群 ◎著

背單字沒這麼難啦！

不是記不住單字，是不懂得怎麼運用聯想力！

特別企劃**4**大主題，分**48**個單元，教你

這樣看：主題分類方便搜尋，Upgrade聰明生活力！

這樣唸：外師親自錄製MP3，不怕開口說英文！

這樣用：搭配超貼切例句，活用單字！

一本一次抓住
【人與生活】、【地點與大自然】、【教育與流行】、【食物與健康】
的英文字彙書！

MP3

編者序

　　一般大家比較熟悉的英文單字背法即是：買一本單字書，由 A 到 Z 依序往下背的填鴨式記憶法。往往很多讀者會遇到的情況是，單字記住了，卻不曉得該如何用、在哪裡用。更有人是，看到一半，覺得單字太多、時間不夠，索性放棄。

　　本書整理了 4 大方向的與職場相關的常用單字，依主題分類，讓讀者輕鬆吸收英文字彙，另附美籍老師錄製的 MP3，方便讀者邊聽、邊看、邊學、邊記憶。期許讀者學英文之路順遂。

編輯部

Contents

目次

主題 2　地點與大自然

主題 3　教育與流行

主題 4 食物與健康

主題 1
People & Life
人與生活

Unit 01

Relationship 關係

Track 01

1 family [ˋfæməlɪ] *n.* 家，家庭

There are four people in my family.

我家裡有四口人。

family name 姓

family tree 家譜

2 folk [fok] *n.* 人們，家屬，親屬；雙親

They are the best folks that I have ever met.

他是我遇過最好的人。

3 father [ˋfɑðə] *n.* 父親

My father reads the newspaper every morning.

我爸爸每天早上看報紙。

Father Christmas 聖誕老人

father-in-law 岳父，公公

4 mother [ˋmʌðə] *n.* 母親

My father and mother went for a walk.

我爸媽去散步了。

mother tongue 本國語

at your mother's knee 當你還很小的時候

5 mama　['mɑmə]　*n.*　媽媽

Mama did the dishes this morning.

媽媽今天早上洗碗。

6 cherish　['tʃɛrɪʃ]　*vt.*　珍愛；懷有（感情）

A mother cherishes her baby.

母親疼愛孩子。

【同】treasure, value

7 brother　['brʌðɚ]　*n.*　兄，弟

I always confused him with his twin brother.

我總分不清他和他的孿生兄弟。

younger brother 弟弟

elder brother 哥哥

8 brotherhood　['brʌðɚ,hʊd]　*n.*　手足情誼，兄弟關係

He believes in the brotherhood of all peoples.

他相信各民族間都應四海之內皆兄弟。

-hood 狀態

childhood 童年

falsehood 謬誤

9 sister　['sɪstɚ]　*n.*　姐，妹

She is my sister.

她是我姐姐。

older / elder sister 姊姊

younger sister 妹妹

10 grandfather　[ˋɡrænd͵faðɚ]　n.　祖父；外祖父

Although his grandfather was a nobleman, he was very poor.

儘管他的祖父是貴族，他卻非常窮困。

Grandpa is my father's father.

爺爺是爸爸的爸爸。

11 descendant　[dɪˋsɛndənt]　n.　子孫，後裔；弟子

He is a descendant of Queen Victoria.

他是維多利亞女王的後裔。

12 uncle　[ˋʌŋk!]　n.　叔，伯，舅，姨父

Your uncle is very sick.

你的叔叔病得很厲害。

Uncle Wang 王叔叔

13 aunt　[ænt]　n.　伯母，嬸母，姑母

The girl was committed to the care of an aunt.

這女孩被交給姨母照顧。

agony aunt 問答專欄（讀者問答專欄解答困擾的阿姨）

14 nephew　[ˋnɛfju]　n.　侄子，外甥

Her nephew was born this summer.

她的姪子這個夏天出生了。

15 **niece**　　[nis]　　*n.*　　侄女，甥女

That young girl is his niece.

那個年輕的女孩是他的姪女。

16 **couple**　　[ˋkʌp!]　　*n.*　　一對；夫婦

They are a happy couple.

他們是很美滿的一對。

a newly-married couple 一對新婚夫婦

17 **spouse**　　[spaʊz]　　*n.*　　配偶，夫妻

Jobs are available for spouses on campus and in the community.

校園裡和社區裡有配偶可做的工作。

【同】husband, wife, partner, mate

18 **intimate**　　[ˋɪntəmɪt]　　*adj.*　　親密的；個人的

My best friend and I became intimate when we met at first sight.

我和我最好的朋友一見如故。

【同】close

19 **dear**　　[dɪr]　　*adj.*　　昂貴的，高價的

The accident cost her dear.

這次事故使她損失慘重。

hold one's life dear 珍重生命

20 darling　[ˋdɑrlɪŋ]　*n.*　親愛的人；寵兒

My darling, you are adorable.

親愛的，你真迷人。

21 together　[təˋgɛðɚ]　*adv.*　一起

They traveled together.

他們一起旅遊。

22 concord　[ˋkɑnkɔrd]　*n.*　和睦，公約

Those neighboring states have lived in concord for centuries.

那些毗鄰的國家幾個世紀以來一直和睦相處。

【同】agreement, harmony

【反】discord

23 harmony　[ˋhɑrmənɪ]　*n.*　調合，協調，和諧

Her tastes are in harmony with mine.

她的愛好和我相同。

24 communicate　[kəˋmjunə͵ket]　*vi.*　*vt.*　通信；通話

I like to communicate with my family.

我喜歡和我的家人溝通。

【同】converse, talk, telephone

25 interaction　[͵ɪntəˋrækʃən]　*n.*　相互作用；干擾

Students should have more interactions with their instructors.

學生應該與他們的老師多一些互動。

主題 1

26 faith　　[feθ]　*n.*　信任，信心；信仰

Nothing could extinguish my faith in you.

沒有什麼能使我喪失對你的信心。

keep faith with 對⋯守信用

place (put) one's faith in 相信

27 forgive　　[fəˋgɪv]　*vt.*　原諒，饒恕，寬恕

Will you forgive my mistake?

你能原諒我的錯誤嗎？

forgive sb. for doing sth. 原諒某人做的某事

28 secret　　[ˋsikrɪt]　*n.*　秘密

Do not tell anyone this secret, or you'll get in trouble.

別告訴任何人這個秘密，不然你會惹禍上身。

29 faithful　　[ˋfeθfəl]　*adj.*　忠誠的；如實的

The couple is faithful to each other.

這對伴侶對彼此忠誠。

30 regard　　[rɪˋgɑrd]　*vt.*　把⋯看作；尊敬

I hold her in high regard.

我很尊敬她。

The students regarded him as a fool.

那些學生認為他是個傻瓜。

Unit
02

Expression 表達

Track 02

1 **attract**　[əˋtrækt]　*vt.*　吸引；引起，誘惑

The concert attracted lots of people this year.

今年的音樂會吸引很多人。

attract sb. from sw. 從某處吸引某人

attract one's attention 吸引某人的注意力

2 **oppose**　[əˋpoz]　*vt.*　反對；反抗

He opposed his children's decision to move out.

他反對他的小孩搬出家門的決定。

oppose (sb. / st.) doing sth. → oppose changing the law 反
對修法

3 **persuade**　[pɚˋswed]　*vt.*　勸說；說服

She persuaded me to buy it.

她說服我買下了它。

The clerk persuades me to buy the expensive shoes.

那個店員說服我買下那昂貴的鞋。

persuade sb. (to do st.) 說服某人（做某事）

persuade sb. into (doing) sth. 說服某人（做某事）

4 **convince**　[kənˋvɪns]　*vt.*　使確信，使信服

I was convinced that Peter knew the fact, but he didn't tell us.
我確信 Peter 知道事實，但他沒有告訴我們。

5 promise [`prɑmɪs] *n.* 諾言 *vt.* *vi.* 答應

Give me your promise that you won't make the same
mistake again.
跟我保證你不會再犯同樣的錯誤。

I can promise you.
我可以跟你保證。

promise to do sth. 答應做某事
keep one's promise 履行諾言

6 understand [ˌʌndɚˈstænd] *vt.* 懂；獲悉 *vi.* 懂得

I don't understand what you are saying.
我不知道你在說什麼。

understand each other 彼此理解
make sb. understand sth. 使某人理解某事

7 imitate [`ɪməˌtet] *vt.* 模仿，仿效；仿製

He can imitate his boss perfectly.
他能惟妙惟肖地模仿他的老闆。

8 prefer [prɪˈfɝ] *vt.* 寧可，寧願

Bradon prefers not to think about the future.
Bradon 寧可先不去想未來的事。

would prefer sth. 比較喜歡某東西
prefer sb. not to do sth. 寧願某人不做某事

9　express　[ɪk`sprɛs]　*vt.*　表示　*n.*　快車，快遞

I can't express how grateful I am.

我說不出我有多麼感激。

express one's satisfaction 表示對⋯⋯的滿意

10　fascinate　[`fæsn,et]　*vt.*　迷住　*vi.*　迷人

The girl was fascinated by his talent.

這女孩被他的才華吸引住了。

11　beguile　[bɪ`gaɪl]　*v.*　欺騙，誘騙

John beguiled her into lending him her notes.

約翰騙她把筆記借給了他。

be beguiled by one's appearance 被某人的外表所欺騙

12　inspire　[ɪn`spaɪr]　*vt.*　鼓舞；給⋯⋯以靈感

The story inspired us to chase our own dreams bravely.

那故事鼓舞了我們勇敢追求自己的夢想。

13　thank　[θæŋk]　*v.*　謝謝

Thanks for asking me.

謝謝你的關心。

Thank you for having me.

謝謝你邀請我。

14　attempt　[ə`tɛmpt]　*vt.*　嘗試，試圖　*n.*　企圖

My first attempt at apple pie tasted terrible.

我首次試做的蘋果派難吃極了。

make an attempt at sth. 試圖、企圖、打算

make an attempt to do sth. 試圖、力圖、努力

15 scream　[skrim]　*vi.*　尖叫；呼嘯

The boy was screaming with pain.

這男孩痛得尖叫起來。

16 regret　[rɪ`grɛt]　*vt.*　*vi.*　遺憾，抱歉

He regretted not having studied harder.

他後悔沒有更加用功地學習。

We regret that we are not able to help you.

我們後悔我們沒能幫你。

17 encourage　[ɪn`kɝɪdʒ]　*vt.*　鼓勵，支援，助長

His success encouraged them to try the same thing.

他的成功鼓勵他們試做同樣的事。

encourage sb. to do sth. 鼓勵某人做某事

encourage sb. 激勵某人

18 explain　[ɪk`splen]　*vt.*　*vi.*　解釋，說明

He explained the reason why he was late for the class.

他解釋他上課遲到的原因。

explain sth. to sb. 給某人解釋某事

explain to sb. 向某人解釋

19 fear　[fɪr]　*n.*　害怕；擔心　*vt.*　害怕

She has a great fear of snakes.

她對蛇有極大的恐懼。

shock with fear 嚇一大跳，震驚

20 praise [prez] *vt.* *n.* 讚揚，表揚

The professor praised her for her intelligence.

教授讚揚了她的機智。

Everyone praised the book.

每個人都稱讚這本書。

21 tribute [`trɪbjut] *n.* 貢物；獻禮，貢獻

Many neighboring countries had to send yearly tribute to ChangAn.

許多鄰近國家不得不每年向長安進貢。

22 gratitude [`grætə,tjud] *adj.* 感激，感謝，感恩

We owe you a debt of gratitude for your help.

對於你的幫忙，我們感恩不盡。

23 appreciate [ə`priʃɪ,et] *vt.* 感激；欣賞

We appreciated your efforts and kindness.

我們感激你的努力與好意。

24 affliction [ə`flɪkʃən] *n.* 痛苦，折磨

His stomachache is a great affliction to him.

胃痛對他來說是個很大的折磨。

25 astonish [ə`stanɪʃ] *vt.* 使驚訝

She was astonished at the news of the accident.

聽到意外的消息，她感到驚訝。

26 reflect   [rɪˋflɛkt]   *vt.*   反射；反映；思考

My sister's sad looks reflected the thought passing through her mind.

我妹妹憂戚的面容反映出她內心的想法。

27 contented   [kənˋtɛntɪd]   *adj.*   滿足的，心安的

Happy is he who is contented with what he has.

【諺】知足者常樂。

28 delight   [dɪˋlaɪt]   *n.*   快樂

The little boy ran back home with delight.

這個小男孩興高采烈地跑回家。

take delight in 樂於…，愛好…

to the boy's delight 使那個男孩高興的是

29 gross   [ɡrɒs]   *adj.*   （語言、舉止）粗俗的

Tom regretted very much having said something gross to his friend.

Tom 非常後悔對他的朋友說了一些粗話。

30 puzzle   [ˋpʌz!]   *vt.*   使迷惑；使為難

His recent behavior puzzles me.

他最近的行為使我迷惑不解。

Unit 03

Personality 個性

Track 03

1 ambitious [æm`bɪʃəs] *adj.* 有雄心的；熱望的

She ventured on an ambitious project.

她冒險從事一項極具雄心的計畫。

2 active [`æktɪv] *adj.* 活躍的；積極的

She is active in the party.

她在派對上很活躍。

lead an active life 過著積極的生活

an active man 一個積極的人

3 brave [brev] *adj.* 勇敢的，華麗的

Those brave heroes deserve our worship.

那些勇敢的英雄們值得我們的崇拜。

as brave as a lion 勇猛如雄獅

a brave soldier 一個勇敢的士兵

4 shy [ʃaɪ] *adj.* 易受驚的；害羞的

I remembered I was a shy boy in my childhood.

我記得我童年時是個害羞的男孩。

a shy smile 一個害羞的微笑

5 **charming** [`tʃɑrmɪŋ] *adj.* 迷人的，可愛的

He looks charming.

他看起來很迷人。

在電影，"Shrek" 中，有一個 Prince Charming 的角色，他是個很自戀的人，一直以為自己應該是拯救 Fiona 的英雄，沒想到 Fiona 竟被 Shrek 拯救，到最後還跟 Shrek 結婚，如果將動畫中的形象和他的名字串連在一起，那這個單字你鐵定忘不掉。

主題 1

6 **cowardly** [`kaʊədlɪ] *adj.* 懦弱的，卑怯的，膽小的

It is cowardly of her not to admit her mistake.

她不承認錯誤就是懦弱的。

coward *n.* 懦夫

7 **cautious** [`kɔʃəs] *adj.* 小心的，謹慎的

He is cautious of telling secrets.

他很謹慎，不會洩漏秘密。

8 **clever** [`klɛvə] *adj.* 機靈的，聰明的

He is a clever kid.

他是一個聰明的孩子。

She's clever at cooking.

她擅長烹調。

be clever with sth. 善於使用某東西

【同】smart, brilliant, bright

9　**brilliant**　[`brıljənt]　*adj.*　光輝的；卓越的

She is brilliant, and organizes her work well.

她很有才華，且工作很有條理。

10　**cruel**　[`kruəl]　*adj.*　殘忍的，殘酷的

The emperor was cruel to his people.

這個皇帝對他的人民很殘酷。

11　**generous**　[`dʒɛnərəs]　*adj.*　慷慨的；寬厚的

He has been very generous.

他一直都很慷慨。

be generous with sth. 對……慷慨

12　**earnest**　[`ɝnɪst]　*adj.*　認真的，誠懇的

Teachers love earnest pupils.

老師喜歡認真的學生。

13　**generosity**　[ˌdʒɛnəˋrɑsətı]　*n.*　慷慨，寬宏大量

Thanks for your generosity.

感謝您的慷慨。

14　**frank**　[fræŋk]　*adj.*　坦白的，直率的

Alice will be frank with you.

Alice 下課將會坦白跟你說。

to be frank with you 跟你坦白說

15 friendly [ˈfrɛndlɪ] *adj.* 友好的

She is friendly with them.

她對他們很友好。

16 careless [ˈkɛrlɪs] *adj.* 粗心的

He's careless in everything.

他事事粗心。

make a careless mistake 犯了一個粗心錯誤

17 haughty [ˈhɔtɪ] *adj.* 傲慢的，輕蔑的

She had a superior, haughty attitude toward other people.

她對其他人有優越、傲慢態度。

18 proud [praʊd] *adj.* 驕傲的；自豪的

I'm proud to be your friend.

做你的朋友我感到驕傲。

be proud of sth. 對某事感到驕傲

be proud of sb. 對某人感到驕傲

19 stubborn [ˈstʌbɚn] *adj.* 頑固的；頑強的

The defenders put up a stubborn resistance.

防守將士進行了頑強的抵抗。

20 honest [ˈɑnɪst] *adj.* 誠實的；可敬的

Always be honest, and never lie.

永遠誠實，別說謊。

to be honest 老實說

【反】dishonest

21 **kind**　[kaɪnd]　*adj.*　仁慈的；和藹的

They are very kind to me.
他們對我很好。
kind-hearted 心地善良的
different kinds of 各種各樣的

22 **lively**　[ˋlaɪvlɪ]　*adj.*　活潑的，有生氣的

The jazz band played a lively tune.
爵士樂團演奏了一支活潑的曲調。
a lively girl 活潑的女孩
a lively dance 輕盈的舞蹈

23 **enthusiastic**　[ɪnˌθjuzɪˋæstɪk]　*adj.*　熱情的，熱心的

Angela is very enthusiastic about the project.
安琪拉對該項計畫十分熱心。
【同】zealous, passionate
【反】cool, indifferent

24 **intelligent**　[ɪnˋtɛlədʒənt]　*adj.*　聰明的；理智的

It is hard for some intelligent people to keep modest.
對有些聰明人來說，保持謙虛挺困難的。
【同】clever, bright, smart, alert

25 practical [ˋpræktɪkl] *adj.* 實際的；應用的

Your plan is practical and workable.

你的計劃是實際又可行的。

He's studying practical English.

他正在學習實用的英語。

26 reliable [rɪˋlaɪəbl] *adj.* 可靠的，可信賴的

Gary found this to be a reliable brand of cell phone.

Gary 發現這個品牌的手機相當可靠。

27 selfish [ˋsɛlfɪʃ] *adj.* 自私的，利己的

Stay away from him. He is a selfish guy.

離他遠一點，他是一個自私的人。

selfish behavior 自私的行為

28 hospitable [ˋhɑspɪtəbl] *adj.* 宜人的，有利的；好客的

My grandpa is always hospitable.

我爺爺總是很好客。

29 loyal [ˋlɔɪəl] *adj.* 忠誠的，忠心的

He is loyal to his wife.

他對妻子很忠誠。

30 strict [strɪkt] *adj.* 嚴格的；嚴謹的

Our manager is very strict with us.

我們的經理對我們要求很嚴格。

Unit 04

Feeling 感覺

 Track 04

1 joy [dʒɔɪ] *n.* 歡樂；高興

Success brought her joy.
成功帶給她喜悅。

to one's joy 令人高興的是
full of joy 充滿了愉快

2 happiness [ˋhæpɪnɪs] *n.* 幸福，幸運；快樂

Never hesitate when the happiness knocks on your door.
當幸福來敲門時，千萬別猶豫。

3 satisfaction [ˌsætɪsˋfækʃən] *n.* 滿意；樂事；賠償

Your satisfaction is guaranteed.
包你滿意。

I had a feeling of satisfaction when the work was finished.
當工作結束的時候，我有一種滿意的感覺。

4 sorrow [ˋsaro] *n.* 悲痛；遺憾

Jim felt sorrow at the death of his dog.
Jim 對於他狗狗死掉感到悲痛。

the joys and sorrows of childhood 童年的開心與悲傷的事

5 **sadness** [`sædnɪs] *n.* 悲痛，悲哀

Sadness prevailed in her mind.

她心中充滿悲痛。

【同】burden, encumber, lumber

6 **freedom** [`fridəm] *n.* 自由；自主

She pursued freedom in her lifetime.

她畢生追尋自由。

freedom of speech 言論自由

7 **love** [lʌv] *vt.* 愛，喜歡 *n.* 愛

Her love for him never wavered.

她對他的愛從未動搖過。

a love of learning 愛好學習

be (fall) in love with sb. 愛上某人

8 **trust** [trʌst] *vt.* *n.* 信任

I have no trust in him.

我不信任他。

trust sb. 相信某人

make sb. trust sth. 使某人相信某事

9 **crazy** [`krezɪ] *adj.* 瘋狂的，荒唐的

He is crazy about her.

他狂熱地愛上她。

go crazy 發瘋；失去理智

【同】mad, insane, ridiculous

10 **disappointment**　[,dɪsə`pɔɪntmənt]　*n.*　失望；沮喪

To his disappointment, he doesn't get the job.

令他失望的是，他沒得到這份工作。

disappoint　*vt.*　使失望

11 **depress**　[dɪ`prɛs]　*vt.*　使沮喪；按下

He was depressed by his defeat.

失敗讓他沮喪。

12 **relief**　[rɪ`lif]　*n.*　寬慰；欣慰

Helen breathed a sigh of relief after hearing the good news.

在 Helen 聽到消息後，她安心了。

13 **dislike**　[dɪs`laɪk]　*vt.*　*n.*　不喜愛，厭惡

If you behave like that, you'll get yourself disliked.

如果你的行為那樣，你會讓人厭惡的。

14 **hate**　[het]　*vt.*　恨，憎恨；不喜歡

They hate each other.

他們彼此憎恨。

hate doing sth. 恨做某事

hate to do sth. 不喜歡做某事，討厭做某事

15 **detest**　[dɪ`tɛst]　*v.*　深惡，憎惡

I detest all affectation.

我厭惡一切矯揉造作的行為。

16 **threaten** [ˋθrɛtn] *vt.* *vi.* 威脅，恐嚇

The employees were threatened with dismissal if they did not work overtime.

員工受到威脅說，如果他們不加班，就會被解雇。

threaten sb. 威脅某人

17 **enjoy** [ɪnˋdʒɔɪ] *vt.* 享受；欣賞，喜愛

I very much enjoyed the party.

我非常喜歡這次聚會。

enjoy oneself 過得愉快，玩得高興（愉快）

enjoy doing sth. 喜歡做某事

18 **hope** [hop] *n.* *vt.* 希望

I hope that Emily will succeed in her business.

我希望 Emily 生意成功。

hope to do sth. 希望做某事

19 **wish** [wɪʃ] *vt.* *n.* 希望；祝願

Do you wish when you see a shooting star?

你看見流星時會許願望嗎？

wish sb. to do sth. 要某人做某事

wish sb. success 祝某人成功

20 **dream** [drim] *vt.* *vi.* 做夢 *n.* 夢想

I believed that one day my dream will come true.

我相信有一天我的夢想會成真。

21 surprise [sə`praɪz] *n.* 驚奇，詫異

To my surprise, his team had a 20-game winning streak.

出乎我意料之外，他隊伍獲得 20 連勝。

a surprise for sb. 給某人的驚奇

taken by surprise 使吃驚

22 exhaust [ɪg`zɔst] *vt.* 使筋疲力盡；用盡

My father is completely exhausted.

我父親精疲力竭。

23 confident [`kɑnfədənt] *n.* 確信的，自信的

For my own part, maintaining a nice appearance keeps me confident.

對我而言，注重儀表讓我有自信。

24 frustrate [`frʌs,tret] *vt.* 挫敗；使無效

The young guy was frustrated by the failure.

這個年輕人因為失敗而灰心喪氣。

25 lonely [`lonlɪ] *adj.* 孤獨的；荒涼的

When his girlfriend broke up with him, he felt sad and lonely.

當他的女朋友跟他分手，他覺得難過且孤單。

【同】alone, friendless, lonesome

主題 1

26 jealous　[`dʒɛləs]　*adj.*　嫉妒的；猜疑的

She is jealous of her classmate's beauty and success.

她嫉妒她同學的美貌與成功。

make sb. jealous 讓某人吃醋

27 curious　[`kjʊrɪəs]　*adj.*　好奇的，奇妙的

The kid is always curious about new knowledge.

這個孩子總是對新知識感到好奇。

28 lucky　[`lʌkɪ]　*adj.*　幸運的，僥倖的

How lucky you are! She accepted your proposal.

你好幸運！她接受你的求婚。

29 excite　[ɪk`saɪt]　*vt.*　使興奮；使激動

I am so excited about this project.

我對這個計畫非常興奮。

The fairy tale excited the little girl.

童話故事使這個小女孩非常激動。

cxciting　*adj.*　令人興奮的

30 extremely　[ɪk`strimlɪ]　*adv.*　極端，極其，非常

She is extremely stingy and narrow-minded.

她極度吝嗇又心胸狹窄。

Body 身體

Track 05

1 eye [aɪ] *n.* 眼睛；眼力；鑒賞力

You're only a kid in my eye.

在我眼裡你不過是個小孩。

2 eyelid [`aɪ,lɪd] *n.* 眼瞼，眼皮

Her eyelids are pink with eye shadow.

她的眼皮塗上粉紅色的眼影。

3 see [si] *vt.* *vi.* 看

He was seen to come out.

有人看見他走出來。

4 view [vju] *n.* 視野

His view of life is different from yours.

他的人生觀與你的不同。

have strong political views 有強烈的政治看法

5 hand [hænd] *n.* 手

She made this beautiful card with her own two hands.

她親手做這張美麗的問候卡。

with one's bare hands 赤手

6 touch [tʌtʃ] *vt.* 觸摸；接觸

I told you not to touch my things!

我告訴過你，別動我的東西！

touch on 涉及，談及

get in touch with sb. 與某人聯繫

7 finger [ˋfɪŋgɚ] *n.* 手指

He cut his finger while chopping up the vegetables.

他在切菜時割傷手指頭。

let sth. slip (through your fingers) 錯過機會

8 ankle [ˋæŋk!] *n.* 踝，踝節部

The doctor ordered the man who had sprained his ankle to keep off it for a few days.

醫生命令那扭傷足踝的人靜養幾天。

9 leg [lɛg] *n.* 腿

Anthony has a severe pain in his leg.

Anthony 的腿劇烈疼痛。

break a leg 祝福，祝……成功

cost / pay an arm and a leg 花很多錢

10 attractive [əˋtræktɪv] *adj.* 有吸引力的

Ice cream is attractive to children.

霜淇淋對孩子們非常有吸引力。

11 **muscle** [`mʌs!] *n.* 肌肉

Michael shows his strong muscles in the gym.

Michael 在健身房展現他強壯的肌肉。

relax one's tense muscles 放鬆某人緊繃的肌肉

12 **strong** [strɔŋ] *adj.* 堅固的；強有力的

James is strong enough to carry the heavy box.

James 夠強壯能搬那個很重的箱子。

13 **jump** [dʒʌmp] *vi.* 跳；暴漲 *vt.* 跳過

The loud bang made me jump.

砰的一聲巨響嚇了我一跳。

14 **stand** [stænd] *vi.* 站；坐落 *n.* 架，台

They all stand in line to buy the limited sneakers.

他們全部排隊買限量球鞋。

stand for 代表，象徵

15 **toe** [to] *n.* 腳趾，足尖

I've stubbed my toe on a chair.

我的腳趾踢到椅子了。

dig your heels / toes in 拒絕做某事或改變你對某事的決定

16 brain   [bren]   *n.*   腦（子）；腦力，智能

Jennifer has more brains than any of us, so she can easily pass the exam.

Jennifer 比你我都聰明，所以她能輕易通過考試。

use one's brain 用腦筋

have no brain 沒有智慧

17 head   [hɛd]   *n.*   頭

He was hit by the dodge ball on the head during the game.

他在比賽時被躲避球打到頭。

keep / have your head straight 保持你的頭腦清醒

have a headache 頭痛

18 think   [θɪŋk]   *vt.*   想；想要；認為

I don't think this film can break the box office record.

我不相信這部電影會打破票房紀錄。

think hard 努力思考

think it over 仔細考慮考慮它

19 nose   [noz]   *n.*   鼻子

She kept blowing her nose this afternoon.

她今天下午一直擤鼻子。

running nose 流鼻水

blow one's nose 擤鼻子

20 **breathe**　[brið]　*vi.*　*vt.*　呼吸

This young man is still breathing; we should take him to the hospital as soon as possible.

這個年輕人還在呼吸；我們應該儘快送他到醫院去。

stop breathing 停止呼吸

21 **chin**　[tʃɪn]　*n.*　頦，下巴

She is care for her double chin, and feels uneasy.

她很在意她的雙下巴，且感到不自在。

22 **cheek**　[tʃik]　*n.*　面頰，臉蛋

A bullet grazed his cheek.

子彈擦傷了他的面頰。

Tears ran down her cheeks.

淚水流落她的雙頰。

23 **beard**　[bɪrd]　*n.*　鬍鬚，絡腮鬍子

Why don't you shave your beard off?

你怎麼不把鬍子刮掉？

24 **shave**　[ʃev]　*vt.*　剃，刮　*vi.*　修面

My father shaves off his beard every day.

我爸爸天天刮鬍子。

25 **razor**　[`rezɚ]　*n.*　剃刀

My father shaved his face with the new electric razor.

我父親用新的電動刮鬍刀刮他的鬍子。

26 cut [kʌt] *vt.* 切；割；砍

The rumor cut their relationship eventually.

謠言最終切斷了他們的關係。

cut off 切斷，中斷，砍掉

cut through 鑿穿，剪開

27 hair [hɛr] *n.* 頭髮

She has beautiful long hair.

她有一頭漂亮的長頭髮。

She brushes her hair.

她梳頭髮。

have a haircut 剪頭

28 comb [kom] *n.* 梳子

My hair needs a good comb.

我的頭髮需要好好梳理一番。

comb one's hair 梳頭

29 sleek [slik] *v.* （使）光滑　*adj.* 光滑的，整潔的

The dog looked very sleek.

這隻狗的毛很光滑。

30 neck [nɛk] *n.* 頸，脖子

The neck of a shirt gets dirty easily.

襯衫領口很容易弄髒。

neck to neck 齊頭並進

Clothes 服裝

Track 06

1 **pants**　[pænts]　*n.*　褲子；男用短襯褲

He bought two pairs of pants online.

他在網路上買了兩條褲子。

2 **trousers**　[ˋtraʊzəz]　*n.*　長褲

You have to wash your trousers.

你必須洗你的長褲。

【同】pants, slacks, jeans, denims

3 **jeans**　[dʒinz]　*n.*　斜紋布，牛仔褲

She wants to buy a pair of light blue jeans.

她想要買一條淺藍色的牛仔褲。

denim 是一種耐用的棉質布料，通常用來做牛仔褲。

4 **fit**　[fɪt]　*vt.*　*vi.*　適合，合身

This dress doesn't fit you at all.

這件洋裝一點也不適合你。

be fit for sb. to do sth. 某人做某事是適合的

be fit for 適合於……

5 **loose** [lus] *adj.* 鬆的；寬鬆的

I usually wore loose garments at home.

我在家總是穿著寬鬆的衣服。

a loose tooth 一顆鬆動的牙齒

a loose button 一個鬆動的鈕扣

6 **tight** [taɪt] *adv.* 緊緊地 *adj.* 牢固的

The jeans are too tight for me.

這條牛仔褲對我來說太緊了。

She's wearing a tight dress.

她穿著緊身連衣裙。

7 **expand** [ɪkˋspænd] *vt.* 擴大；使膨脹

Metals expand when they are heated.

金屬遇熱則膨脹。

【同】bloat, bulge, swell

【反】shrink

8 **shrink** [ʃrɪŋk] *vi.* 收縮；縮小；退縮

She had a tendency to shrink up whenever attention was focused on her.

當別人注意她時，她就會退縮到一旁。

【同】contract, shorten, dwindle

【反】swell, expand

9　shirt　[ʃɝt]　*n.*　（男式）襯衫

Will you stitch a button on this shirt?

請你在這件襯衫上釘一顆紐扣好嗎？

a cotton shirt 一件棉質的襯衫

wear a shirt and tie 穿西裝打領帶

10　collar　[`kɑlɚ]　*n.*　衣領，項圈

What size collar is this shirt?

這襯衣領子的尺寸是多少？

blue-collar worker 藍領

white-collar worker 白領

11　skirt　[skɝt]　*n.*　女裙

I really like that red skirt.

我真的很喜歡那件紅裙子。

12　dress　[drɛs]　*n.*　衣服；連衣裙

My sister wears a beautiful white dress.

我妹妹穿了一件很漂亮的白色洋裝。

dress up 打扮起來，穿上

dress oneself as... 把某人自己扮成……

13　compliment　[`kɑmpləmənt]　*n.*　問候　*vt.*　讚美，祝賀

My boyfriend complimented me on my new outfit.

我男朋友稱讚我的新衣服。

14 blouse　[blaʊz]　*n.*　女襯衫；童衫；罩衫

She is wearing a white blouse today.

今天她穿了一件白色襯衫。

a silk blouse 一件絲質罩衫

15 veil　[vel]　*n.*　面紗，面罩；遮蔽物

Most Muslim women wear veils in public places.

大多數穆斯林婦女在公共場所都戴著面紗。

a bridal veil 新娘頭紗

draw a veil over sth. 避免談論某事

16 scarf　[skɑrf]　*n.*　圍巾，頭巾；領帶

I got a new scarf on my birthday.

我生日時收到一條新圍巾。

此名詞為 "f" 結尾，複數要去 "f" 加 ves，變成 "scarves"。

17 silk　[sɪlk]　*n.*　（蠶）絲；絲織品，綢

This beautiful dress is made of silk.

這件美麗的洋裝是用絲做成的。

18 sock　[sɑk]　*n.*　短襪

There is a hole in my sock.

我的襪子上有個洞。

blow / knock someone's socks off 讓某人很驚訝或印象深刻

19 **shoe** [ʃu] *n.* 鞋

Kevin can't wait to show off his expensive shoes to his friends.

Kevin 等不及給他的朋友看他昂貴的鞋子。

shoe polish 鞋油

shoe brush 鞋刷

20 **belt** [bɛlt] *n.* 帶，腰帶；皮帶；區

He bought a new belt for his wedding.

他為他的婚禮買了一條新皮帶。

21 **adjust** [əˋdʒʌst] *vt.* 調整，調節；校正

You need to adjust your attitude towards work, or you'll be in a mess.

你必須調整你的工作態度，不然你會一團糟。

22 **loosen** [ˋlusn] *vi.* 變鬆

He loosened his tie after work.

他下班後鬆開領帶。

23 **queer** [kwɪr] *adj.* 奇怪的，古怪的

Her queer way of talking made people stay away from her.

她古怪的說話方式讓人們遠離她。

24 **simplicity** [sɪmˋplɪsətɪ] *n.* 簡單，簡易；樸素

The first lady prefers to dress with elegant simplicity.

第一夫人喜愛穿著樸素雅致。

be simplicity itself 非常簡單

25 costume [ˈkɑstjum] *n.* 服裝，劇裝

She changed into her best costume for the dancing party.
她換上她最好的服裝參加舞會。

26 coat [kot] *n.* 外套，上衣；表皮

I feel a little cold right now. Could you bring me my coat?
我覺得現在有一點冷。你能幫我帶我的外套嗎？
a long winter coat 一件冬季長大衣
put on one's coat 穿上衣服

27 suit [sut] *n.* 一套（衣服）

He is wearing a black suit.
他穿著一套黑西裝。

28 corset [ˈkɔrsɪt] *n.* 緊身衣

Women don't wear corsets nowadays.
現在婦女不再穿緊身衣了。

29 wig [wɪg] *n.* 假髮

Judges wear wigs in court.
法官開庭時戴假髮。

30 hat [hæt] *n.* 帽子

She always wears a hat when she goes shopping.
她逛街時總是戴著一頂帽子。
take off one's hat 脫帽
put on one's hat 戴上帽子

Unit 07　Daily Life 日常生活

Track 07

1　**walk**　[wɔk]　*vi.*　*n.*　走，步行

I walked home after school every day.
我每天放學走路回家。
walk all the way 走一路

2　**babble**　[ˋbæb!]　*v.*　說蠢話，牙牙學語

The baby babbled for hours.
那嬰孩牙牙學語了好幾個小時。

3　**hear**　[hɪr]　*v.*　聽見，聽

I heard him say so.
我聽到他這麼說過。
hear of 聽說…
hear about 聽說…

4　**push**　[pʊʃ]　*vt.*　推，逼迫　*vi.*　推

He pushed the door rudely.
他粗魯地推開門。
push sth. out 把某東西推出去
push over 推倒；刮倒

5 pull [pʊl] *vt.* 拉，拖；拉，拉力

The door pulled open.

門拉開了。

pull up 停下來，靠岸

pull... up from 拉起，拉上來

主題 1

6 tie [taɪ] *vt.* （用繩等）繫，栓

My younger sister tied the ribbon in a bow.

我妹妹把緞帶繫成一個蝴蝶結。

tie the horse to a post 將馬拴在柱上

tie sth. to sw. 把某東西拴到某地方

7 take [tek] *v.* 拿

My friend took me to this restaurant.

我朋友帶我去這家餐廳。

8 give [gɪv] *v.* 給予

He gave me the flu.

他把流感傳給我了。

動詞三態：give, gave, given

9 write [raɪt] *vt.* 書寫；寫　*vi.* 寫

I've been writing for three hours.

我已經寫了三個小時了。

write notes 做筆記

10 read [rid] *v.* 讀

I can read French but I can't speak it.

我能看懂法文但不會說。

read out to sb. 給某人讀

read about sb. 讀關於某人的書

11 memorize [`mɛmə,raɪz] *vt.* 記住

She can memorize facts very quickly.

她能很快記住許多資料。

12 mention [`mɛnʃən] *vt.* *n.* 提到，說起

She mentioned that you want to apply for the job.

她提到你想申請那份工作。

above-mentioned 上面提到的

below-mentioned 下面提到的

13 describe [dɪ`skraɪb] *vt.* 形容；描寫，描繪

She describes the situation vividly.

她把情況描述得栩栩如生。

describe books as "hard-to-put-down"

描寫為放不下的書

write a letter home describing sth.

給家裡寫一封信描寫某事

14 join [dʒɔɪn] *vt.* 加入

She joined the study group this semester.

她這學期加入讀書會。

join...to... 把…連接到…

join in 加入，參加

15 add   [æd]   *vt.*   加，增加

The bad weather added to our difficulties.

壞天氣增加了我們的天氣。

add to 增加

add up to 加起來、總（累）計、意味著

16 subtract   [səb`trækt]   *vt.*   減，減去，去掉

Subtract 3 from 7 and you have 4.

七減三得四。

【同】deduct, take away, remove

17 prepare   [prɪ`pɛr]   *vt.*   *vi.*   準備；預備

He is preparing his speech for the meeting tomorrow.

他正準備明天集會的演說。

prepare a meal 做飯

prepare for 為…做準備

18 applaud   [ə`plɔd]   *vt.*   喝彩；歡呼   *vi.*   歡呼

He was loudly applauded.

他受到熱烈的掌聲歡迎。

【同】acclaim, clap

19 disturb　[dɪs`tɝb]　*vt.*　打擾，擾亂；弄亂

Do not disturb her. She's tired.

別打擾她，她累了。

disturb sb. 打擾某人

20 behave　[bɪ`hev]　*vi.*　表現，舉止；運轉

Behave yourself. This is an official meeting.

注意你的舉止。這是正式會議。

21 deliver　[dɪ`lɪvɚ]　*vt.*　投遞，送交；發表

Newspapers are delivered every day.

報紙每天都送來。

deliver a paper round 到處送報紙

promise to deliver sth. 答應送某東西

22 toss　[tɔs]　*vi.*　翻來覆去

My husband was tossing and turning all night.

我丈夫整夜翻來覆去睡不著。

23 bounce　[baʊns]　*vi.*　反跳，彈起；跳起

The ball hit the wall and bounced off it.

球打在牆上又反彈回來。

24 stride　[straɪd]　*vi.*　大踏步走　*n.*　大步

She strode out of the meeting room angrily.

她氣憤地大步走出會議室。

動詞三態：stride, strode, stridden

25 contact　[`kɑntækt]　*vt.*　使接觸；與…聯繫

I'll contact you this evening.

我今晚會跟你聯絡。

【同】touch, impact, junction

26 scratch　[skrætʃ]　*vt.　vi.　n.*　搔；抓

That cat scratches.

那隻貓會抓傷人。

27 loan　[lon]　*n.*　貸款；暫借　*vt.*　借出

How much interest do they charge on loans?

他們貸款收多少利息？

28 collect　[kə`lɛkt]　*vt.*　收集　*vi.*　收款

Why do you collect stamps?

你為何集郵？

collect sth. for 為…收集某東西

29 detect　[dɪ`tɛkt]　*vt.*　察覺，發覺；偵察

I detected anger in her voice.

我察覺出她說話聲裡含著憤怒。

30 dispose　[dɪ`spoz]　*vi.*　去掉，丟掉；銷毀

I must dispose of the trouble.

我必須擺脫麻煩。

Unit 08

Furniture & Appliances
傢俱 & 器具

Track 08

1　oven　[`ʌvən]　*n.*　爐，灶；烘箱

My grandma took the meat pie out of the oven.

我奶奶從烤箱中拿出肉派。

2　bake　[bek]　*vt.*　烤，烘，焙；燒硬

The bread is baking in the oven.

烤箱裡正在烤麵包。

The cakes will bake very quickly.

蛋糕烤得非常快。

bake bread 烤麵包

3　roast　[rost]　*vt.*　*vi.*　烤，炙，烘

My brother's favorite dish is roast chicken.

我弟弟最喜歡吃的菜是烤雞。

4　broil　[brɔɪl]　*n.*　*v.*　烤，燒；爭吵，怒

They are broiling in the meeting.

他們在會議上怒罵。

5 gas　　[gæs]　　*n.*　　煤氣；氣體；汽油

There are several kinds of gas in the air.

空氣中有幾種氣體。

6 stove　　[stov]　　*n.*　　爐，火爐，電爐

Put the pot on the stove.

把鍋子放在爐子上。

7 stir　　[stɝ]　　*vt.*　　動；撥動；激動　　*n.*　　騷動；混亂

Their relationship caused a stir in our department.

他們的關係在我們部門裡引起了一片混亂。

8 fry　　[fraɪ]　　*vt.*　　油煎，油炸，油炒

The cook fried the potato chips in order to serve the customers.

為了服務顧客，廚師油炸馬鈴薯片。

9 comfort　　[`kʌmfɚt]　　*n.*　　舒適；安慰　　*vt.*　　安慰

He likes his comforts.

他喜歡自己舒適的生活條件。

live in great comfort 非常舒適地生活

10 couch　　[kaʊtʃ]　　*n.*　　睡椅，長沙發椅

Dad is sleeping on the couch.

爸爸在長椅上睡覺。

11 sit [sɪt] *v.* 坐

They sat down quietly.

他們靜靜地坐下。

12 sleep [slip] *v. n.* 睡，睡眠

He didn't sleep well last night.

他昨晚睡不安穩。

go to sleep 入睡；睡著

sleep well 睡得好

13 watch [watʃ] *n.* 手錶

He watched to see what would happen.

他觀察著，看會發生什麼情況。

watch TV 看電視

watch out 小心，提高警覺

14 rock [rɑk] *vt.* 搖，使動搖 *vi.* 搖

The trees rocked in the strong wind.

樹在強風中搖動。

15 warm [wɔrm] *adj.* 暖和的

The day was warm and cloudless.

天氣溫暖而晴朗。

warm clothes 可以保暖的衣服

warm-blooded 熱（暖）血的

16 **mattress** [ˋmætrɪs] *n.* 床墊

She kept her books under her mattress.

她將她的書放在床墊下。

17 **ring** [rɪŋ] *n.* 環形物（如圈、環等）

Her boyfriend gave her a ring on their anniversary.

她男朋友在他們的周年紀念日送她一只戒指。

ring off 掛斷電話，住嘴，離開

ring out 打響，拉響，宣佈結果

18 **bell** [bɛl] *n.* 鈴，鐘

Someone's ringing the bell.

有人正在按門鈴。

That's the bell. 鈴響了。

The bell is ringing. 鈴響了

19 **butter** [ˋbʌtɚ] *n.* 黃油；奶油

We spread butter on bread.

我們把奶油塗到麵包上。

spread butter on bread 在麵包上塗奶油

peanut butter 花生醬

20 **jelly** [ˋdʒɛlɪ] *n.* 凍，果子凍；膠狀物

She tried to make jelly on her own.

她嘗試自己做果凍。

21 jar　[dʒɑr]　*n.*　罈子；罐子；缸

We ate a whole jar of jam.

我們吃掉整整一罐果醬。

a jar of jam 一瓶果醬

wine jars 酒瓶

22 pan　[pæn]　*n.*　平底鍋，盤子

I cracked two eggs into the frying pan.

我在平底鍋裡打了兩個雞蛋。

a pan of oil 一鍋油

a pan of water 一鍋水

23 picture　[ˋpɪktʃɚ]　*n.*　圖畫，照片

I had a picture taken this morning.

今天上午我拍了張照。

take a picture 拍一張照片

24 frame　[frem]　*n.*　框架，框子；鉤架

In a silver frame on the table, there is a photograph of her husband.

在桌上的銀相框裡有張她丈夫的照片。

25 wardrobe　[ˋwɔrd͵rob]　*n.*　衣櫃，衣櫥，藏衣室

He heaved the wardrobe up the stairs.

他用力把衣櫃搬上樓了。

【同】cupboard, closet, clothes

26 handy [ˋhændɪ] *adj.* 方便的；手邊的

The invention of the tool is handy to use.
這項工具的發明很方便使用。
【同】available, accessible

27 lamp [læmp] *n.* 燈

Turn off the lamp, please.
請關掉檯燈。
street lamp 街燈
a spirit lamp 酒精燈

28 candlestick [ˋkænd!ˌstɪk] *n.* 蠟燭臺

He likes to collect silver candlesticks.
他喜歡收藏銀蠟燭臺。

29 freeze [friz] *vi.* 凍；結凍 *vt.* 使結冰

When the thermometer is at 0 degrees centigrade, water will freeze.
當溫度計降至攝氏零度時，水便會結冰。
below freezing 冰點以下

30 blend [blɛnd] *vt.* *vi.* *n.* 混合

Which blend of coffee would you like?
你要哪一種混合咖啡？

Entertainment 娛樂

Track 09

1　TV　*n.*　電視

Do you have a color TV set?
你有彩色電視機嗎？

I watched the game on TV.
我在電視上看了那場比賽。

He turned on the TV.
他打開電視。

2　comedy　[`kamədı]　*n.*　喜劇；喜劇場面

We enjoy watching comedies.
我們喜歡看喜劇。

【反】tragedy

3　laugh　[læf]　*vi.*　笑，發笑　*n.*　笑

She laughed at her husband's bad memory.
她對她丈夫的健忘一笑置之。

be laughed at by sb. 被某人嘲笑
laugh at sth. (sb.) 嘲笑某事（某人）

4　drama　[`drɑmə]　*n.*　一齣戲劇，劇本

She is a student of drama.

她攻讀戲劇。

【同】play, show, theater

5 **cry**　[kraɪ]　*vi.*　哭；叫喊

He cried over his wife's death.

他為妻子的去世而哭泣。

Don't cry. 不要哭。

cry for help 大聲呼救

6 **film**　[fɪlm]　*n.*　電影

He made a film about Egypt.

他拍了一部關於埃及的電影。

【同】movie

7 **silent**　[ˋsaɪlənt]　*adj.*　沉默的；寂靜無聲的

He is the strong, silent type.

他是個堅強而沉默的人。

8 **color**　[ˋkʌlɚ]　*n.*　顏色，彩色；顏料

This is a color television.

這是一台彩色電視機。

9 **game**　[gem]　*n.*　遊戲，運動，比賽

Let's have a game of cards.

我們玩牌吧。

Olympic games 奧林匹克運動會

10 home [hom] *adv.* 回家，在家 *n.* 家

She left home after high school.

她高中後就離家。

do one's homework 做作業

home town 家鄉

11 actor [ˋæktɚ] *n.* 男演員；演劇的人

Being a successful actor is his dream.

當個成功的演員是他的夢想。

12 idol [ˋaɪd!] *n.* 神像、偶像

She is crazy for Korean idols.

她對韓國偶像狂熱。

13 star [stɑr] *vt.* *vi.* 主演

Angelina Jolie has starred in many films.

安潔莉娜裘莉主演過很多部電影。

a movie star 電影明星

an athletic star 體育明星

14 gossip [ˋgɑsəp] *n.* 閒談；碎嘴子；漫筆

He's a terrible gossip.

他專愛說人閒話。

【同】scandal, rumor

15 entertain [ˌɛntɚˋten] *vt.* 使歡樂；招待

He sang to entertain the audience.

他唱歌以娛樂觀眾。

16 park [pɑrk] *n.* 公園

There are many beautiful parks in this city.
這座城市有很多美麗的公園。
in the park 在公園裡
outside the park 在公園的外面

17 hill [hɪl] *n.* 小山

Climb up the hill, and you'll see the temple.
爬上小山，你就會看到那廟宇。
on the hill 在山上
move into the hills 搬到山裡

18 kite [kaɪt] *n.* 風箏

A little boy is flying a kite in the playground.
一個小男孩在遊樂場上放風箏。

19 glide [glaɪd] *vi.* 滑動；消逝 *n.* 滑行

The skater glided gracefully over the ice.
滑冰者在冰上優雅地滑行。

20 wind [wɪnd] *n.* 風

The north wind is blowing hard.
北風勁吹。
a cold wind 寒風
strong winds 大風

21 **art**　[ɑrt]　*n.*　藝術；美術

It's a unique work of art.

這是獨一無二的藝術作品。

the art of talking 談話術

22 **museum**　[mjuˋzɪəm]　*n.*　博物館

The museum has many ancient cultural relics.

該博物館收藏了很多極其古老的文物。

23 **exhibition**　[ˌɛksəˋbɪʃən]　*n.*　展覽

There is a travel exhibition this weekend

這週末有一個旅遊展。

24 **exhibit**　[ɪgˋzɪbɪt]　*vt.*　顯示；陳列，展覽

Do not touch the exhibits.

不要觸摸展示品。

25 **theater**　[ˋθɪətɚ]　*n.*　戲院，電影院，劇場；全體觀眾

The theater gives two performances a day.

這座劇場一天演出兩場。

London has more theatres than any other British city.

倫敦比別的英國城市有更多的劇院。

26 support　[sə`port]　*vt.*　支撐；支援；維持

Her boyfriend supports her decision.

她男朋友支持她的決定。

turn to one's best friend for support 跑到某人最好的朋友那求助

win nationwide support 贏得了全國的支援

主題 1

27 party　[`pɑrtɪ]　*n.*　聚會

He planned a party for his mother.

他為他的媽媽策劃了一個派對。

to one's birthday party 到某人的生日舞會

a dance party 舞會

28 club　[klʌb]　*n.*　俱樂部；社團

Which club does he want to join?

他想加入哪個社團？

the camera club 攝影俱樂部

29 dine　[daɪn]　*vi.*　吃飯　*vt.*　宴請

My roommate and I decide to dine out tonight.

我和我室友決定今晚出去吃飯。

30 dance　[dæns]　*vi.*　跳舞；搖晃　*n.*　舞

Let's dance to the music.

讓我們隨著音樂跳舞。

come to the dance 參加舞會

Activities 活動

 Track 10

1 climb [klaɪm] *v.* 爬；攀登

My grandparents climb mountains every weekend.
我祖父母每週末都去爬山。
climb stairs 爬樓梯
climb out 爬出

2 steep [stip] *adj.* 險峻的，陡峭的

They rode on the steep hill.
他們騎上陡峭的山岡。

3 mountain [`maʊntn] *n.* 山；山脈

The couple decided to live in the mountains once they got married.
這對情侶決定婚後住在山裡。
a line of mountains 一系列山脈
on the edge of a mountain 在山邊

4 rest [rɛst] *vi. vt.* （使）支撐（在）

Rest the ladder against the wall.
把梯子靠在牆上吧。
take a rest 休息

5 **boot** [but] *n.* 靴子，長靴

I want to buy a pair of boots.
我想要買一雙靴子。

6 **camp** [kæmp] *n.* 野營，營地，兵營

The boys went camping last weekend.
男孩子們上週末去野餐。
light camp fires 點營火
go camping 去野營

7 **rustic** [ˋrʌstɪk] *adj.* 鄉村的，鄉土氣的

She expected to enjoy the rustic peace on her vacation.
她期待度假時享受鄉村的寧靜。

8 **fireside** [ˋfaɪrˏsaɪd] *n.* 爐邊，家庭，一家團圓

My grandma sat by the fireside and knitted scarves.
我奶奶坐在爐邊織圍巾。

9 **around** [əˋraʊnd] *prep.* 在…周圍

My secretary will show you around.
我秘書會帶你四處逛逛。
sit around the table 圍桌而坐

10 **skate** [sket] *v.* 滑冰

He is learning how to skate.
他正在學滑冰。

11 **fall** [fɔl] *n.* *vi.* 落下；跌倒

The city fell to the enemy.

該城失陷了。

fall off 跌落，掉下，從…摔下

fall over 摔倒，翻倒，向前跌倒

12 **play** [ple] *n.* 戲劇，表演；玩耍

We've been to several plays this month.

這個月我們看了好幾場戲。

play in the garden 在花園裡玩

play in the game 參加比賽

13 **child** [tʃaɪld] *n.* 小孩

He's still but a child.

他還是個小孩子。

be one's only child 獨生子（女）

be with child 懷孕

14 **toy** [læf] *n.* 玩具

Jimmy bought a toy car for his son.

吉米買了一台玩具車給他的兒子。

15 **fight** [kraɪ] *n.* 打架 *vi.* 爭吵

They are always fighting over trifles.

他們總是為瑣事吵架。

16 **tumble** [ˋtʌmb!] *vi.* 摔倒，跌倒；打滾

The baby tumbled over and hit her head on the ground.
小嬰兒摔倒，頭撞到地面。

17 **recover** [rɪˋkʌvɚ] *vt.* 重新獲得；挽回

She's now fully recovered from her heart disease.
她的心臟病現在已經完全康復了。
He recovered his health.
他恢復健康了。
be recovered 恢復健康

18 **drive** [draɪv] *vt.* *vi.* 驅趕；駕駛

Could you drive me to the station?
你可以開車送我到車站去嗎？
drive sth. out of sw. 把某東西從某地逐出
drive sb. into 使某人進入…

19 **corner** [ˋkɔrnɚ] *n.* 角；（街道）拐角

A cabinet sits in a corner of the room.
有個櫥櫃在房間的一角。

20 **fast** [fæst] *adv.* 快地 *adj.* 快的

He is a fast reader.
他讀書速度很快。
fastest of all 所有當中最快的
go fast 進展得快

21 **splendor**   [ˋsplɛndɚ]   *n.*   壯麗，輝煌

We admired the splendor of the ocean scenery.

我們讚美這海景的壯麗。

22 **landscape**   [ˋlænd‚skep]   *n.*   風景，景色，景致

That skyscraper is a blot on the landscape.

那棟新建的摩天大樓破壞了此地的景色。

【同】scene, view, prospect

23 **stretch**   [strɛtʃ]   *vt.*   伸展   *vi.*   伸   *n.*   伸展

The beach stretched away into the distance.

沙灘一直延伸到遠方。

24 **active**   [ˋæktɪv]   *adj.*   活躍的；積極的

She is active in the ball.

她在舞會上很活躍。

lead an active life 過著積極的生活

an active man 一個積極的人

25 **race**   [res]   *n.*   比賽；賽跑；賽馬

He spent one hour training for the race every morning.

他每天早上花兩個小時練習賽跑。

26 **flexible**   [ˋflɛksəb!]   *adj.*   易彎曲的；靈活的

That's okay. My schedule is quite flexible.

沒關係。我的時間很彈性。

【同】elastic, bendy

27 **strength** [strɛŋθ] *n.* 力量；力氣

Union is strength.
【諺】團結就是力量。
The guy is a man of great strength.
這個男人是個力氣很大的人。
physical strength 體力

28 **improve** [ɪm`pruv] *vt.* 使更好 *vi.* 改善

You had better improve your speaking skills as soon as possible.
你最好盡快改善你的說話技巧。
improve the way of 改進…的方法

29 **hobby** [`hɑbɪ] *n.* 業餘愛好，癖好

Her hobby is collecting stamps.
她的興趣是收集郵票。

30 **music** [`mjuzɪk] *n.* 音樂

She always listens to music when she is in a bad mood.
她心情不好時總是聽音樂。
pop music 流行音樂
folk music 民間音樂

Time 時間

Track 11

1 hour　[aʊr]　*n.*　小時；時間，時刻

It took her an hour to finish the homework.
她花了一小時完成這項作業。
school hours 授課時間
business hours 營業時間

2 minute　[ˋmɪnɪt]　*n.*　分鐘

I'll be back in a minute.
我馬上就回來。
Just a minute, please.
請等一下。
for a minute or two 一兩分鐘的時間

3 waste　[west]　*n.*　*vt.*　浪費

It's a waste of time to speak to her.
和她說話是浪費時間。

4 save　[sev]　*vt.*　救，挽救

He saved me from drowning.
他救了我，使我免遭溺死。

5 **precious** [`prɛʃəs] *adj.* 珍貴的，寶貴的

He has just sent me the most precious gifts.

他剛剛送我最珍貴的禮物。

6 **money** [`mʌnɪ] *n.* 貨幣；金錢，財富

Time is money.

【諺】時間就是金錢。

make money 賺錢

7 **spend** [spɛnd] *vt.* 用錢，花費；度過

The little girl spent the weekend with her grandparents.

這個小女孩和她的祖父母一起度週末。

spend... doing sth. 花（時間／金錢）…做某事

spend...on+ 名詞（動名詞）

8 **forever** [fə`ɛvə] *adv.* 永遠，總是，老是

You'll never break through yourself if you stay at your comfort zone forever.

如果你一直待在你的舒適圈，就永遠不會突破自我。

9 **instant** [`ɪnstənt] *n.* 瞬間 *adj.* 立即的

The email asked for an instant reply.

這封電子信件要求立即回覆。

10 **immediate** [ɪ`midɪɪt] *adj.* 立即的；直接的

This project demands your immediate response.

這項計畫急需你立即回應。

11 arrive ［əˋraɪv］ *vi.* 到達；來臨；達到

We shall arrive soon after.

我們將隨後很快就到達。

arrive from 從…到達

12 depart ［dɪˋpɑrt］ *vi.* 離開，起程；出發

He is unwilling to depart.

他不情願地離開。

13 late ［let］ *adj.* 遲的　*adv.* 遲，晚

The train was 10 minutes late.

火車晚點了 10 分鐘。

a few days later 幾天以後

later on 晚些時候

14 early ［ˋɝlɪ］ *adv.* 早

We should complete the work early or late.

我們遲早要完成這件工作。

get up early 早起床

early or late 遲早，早晚

15 possible ［ˋpɑsəb!］ *adj.* 可能的

I was wondering if it is possible to change the date for our meeting.

我想知道我們有沒有可能更改開會的日期。

as...as possible 盡可能的

if possible 如果可能的話

16 impossible [ɪmˋpɑsəb!] *adj.* 不可能的，辦不到的

It's impossible to finish the paper this weekend.

這個週末完成論文是不可能的。

make it impossible 使它成為不可能的

主題 1

17 performance [pəˋfɔrməns] *n.* 履行；演出；行為

The evening performance is at seven o'clock.

晚上的演出七點開始。

18 start [stɑrt] *vt.* 開始 *vi.* 出發

The company was started in 1995.

該公司 1995 年創立。

start off 出去旅行，出發，動身

19 finish [ˋfɪnɪʃ] *vt.* 完成，結束 *n.* 結束

Let's finish off the wine.

我們把酒喝完吧。

finish with sb. 和某人斷交

finish doing sth. 結束做某事

20 stop [stɑp] *vt.* 塞住；阻止；停止

His heart has stopped.

他的心臟停止了跳動。

protect sb. from doing sth. 阻止某人不做某事

stop to do sth. 停下來去做別的事

21 **abrupt** [ə`brʌpt] *adj.* 突然的，唐突的，無禮的，不連貫的

The abrupt change of schedule gave me lots of trouble.

行程突然改變給我造成許多麻煩。

22 **smooth** [smuð] *adj.* 光滑的；平靜的

She has smooth skin.

她有光滑的皮膚。

smooth away 克服

make sth. smooth 使某東西光滑

23 **first** [fɝst] *n.* 第一

He was the first to be there.

他是第一個到達那裡的。

at first 起先，開始的時候

first of all 首先，第一

24 **last** [læst] *adj.* 最後的　*adv.* 最後

He left last.

他最後離開。

from last time 從上一次

at the last moment 在最後的時刻

25 **only** [`onlɪ] *adv.* 只

We can only wait and see now.

我們現在只好等等再說。

26 part [part] *n.* 一部分；零件

Parts of the book are interesting.

這本書有幾部分很有意思。

take part in 參加

part-time 業餘時間

27 full [fʊl] *adj.* 滿

The bottle is full of water.

瓶子裡裝滿了水。

have a full meal 飽餐一頓

get full marks 得滿分

28 daily [`delɪ] *adj.* 每日的 *n.* 日報

Take two of the tablets three times daily before meals.

每日三次，每次兩片，飯前服用。

29 weekly [`wiklɪ] *adj.* 每週的 *adv.* 每週

The professor moderated the weekly meeting.

教授主持每週的週會。

30 monthly [`mʌnθlɪ] *adj.* 每月的 *adv.* 每月

We used to subscribe to the monthly magazine.

我們過去訂閱這月刊。

Unit
12

Travel 旅遊

Track 12

1　traveler　[ˋtrævlɚ]　*n.*　旅行者

The traveler wrote down what he encountered on his journey.

這位旅行者寫下他在旅途的遭遇。

2　journey　[ˋdʒɝnɪ]　*n.*　旅行，旅程，路程

It's one day's journey to get the Twelve Apostles.

到十二門徒石是一天的行程。

make a journey to sw. 到某地去旅行

have a good journey 祝旅途愉快

3　vacation　[veˋkeʃən]　*n.*　假期，休假

You need a vacation.

你需要休假。

summer vacation 暑假

be on vacation 休假中

4　holiday　[ˋhɑləˏde]　*n.*　假日，節日；假期

We haven't discussed our holiday plan.

我們還沒有討論假日的計畫。

summer holiday 暑假

winter holiday 寒假

5 map [mæp] *n.* 地圖；圖；天體圖

My father gave me a map when I graduated from elementary school.

我小學畢業時，我爸爸送我一張地圖。

a map of China 一張中國地圖

the map of China 中國的地圖

6 review [rɪ`vju] *vt.* 再檢查 *n.* 複習

She reviewed her notes for the exam.

她為了考試複習筆記。

a review of lessons 複習功課

review the past 回顧過去

7 advice [əd`vaɪs] *n.* 勸告；忠告；意見

I ask for advice for my career plan.

我為我的職涯規劃尋求建議。

a piece of advice 一條建議

some advice 一些建議

8 speed [spid] *n.* 速度

The train soon speeded up.

火車不久就加快了速度。

speed-reading 快速閱讀

speed up 加速，提速，加快速度

9 **limit** [ˋlɪmɪt] *n.* 限度;限制;範圍

We must limit our spending.

我們必須限制我們的開支。

a limited variety of 一種有限的…

limit the number of 限制…的數位

10 **destination** [ˏdɛstəˋneʃən] *n.* 目的地,終點;目標

The destination is in view.

終點已經在望。

11 **hire** [haɪr] *vt.* 租借 *n.* 租用,雇用

Hire a car for the day.

白天租用一輛汽車

prefer to hire sb. 寧願雇用某人

12 **coast** [kost] *n.* 海岸,海濱(地區)

They live in a town along the coast.

他們住在一個沿海的城市裡。

be on the coast 在海岸上

near the coast 在海岸附近

13 **ferry** [ˋfɛrɪ] *n.* 渡船;渡口 *vt.* 運送

We took a ferry to the park.

我們搭渡船去公園。

14 island   [ˋaɪlənd]   *n.*   島；島狀物

Palm trees are everywhere on Hainan Island.

海南島上到處都是椰子樹。

15 amuse   [əˋmjuz]   *vt.*   娛樂；逗⋯樂

The comedian amused the audience.

喜劇演員娛樂觀眾。

16 tan   [tæn]   *n.*   棕褐色   *adj.*   棕黃色的

She is eager to get a tan.

她渴望曬出這樣的棕褐色。

17 sunshine   [ˋsʌn,ʃaɪn]   *n.*   （直射）日光，陽光

She enjoys basking in the sunshine.

她享受沐浴在陽光下。

18 rain   [ren]   *v.*   下雨   *n.*   雨

The match was rained off twice.

比賽因雨而被迫兩次改期。

heavy rain 大雨

chemical rain 化學雨，酸雨

19 traffic   [ˋtræfɪk]   *n.*   交通，街道，車輛

There is a traffic jam downtown.

市中心塞車了。

【同】vehicles, shipping

20 fatigue   [fəˈtig]   *n.*   疲勞，勞累

I am utterly fatigued.

我完全累壞了。

【同】tiredness, weakness

21 motel   [moˈtɛl]   *n.*   汽車遊客旅館

The travelers sat down in the motel near the beach.

旅遊者在海濱附近的汽車旅店住了下來。

22 inn   [ɪn]   *n.*   小旅館，客棧

On our trip to Oxford, we stayed in an inn.

去牛津郡旅行的路上，我們住在一個客棧裡。

23 tavern   [ˈtævɚn]   *n.*   小酒店；客棧

Where is the tavern you have mentioned?

你提過的小酒館在哪裡？

24 reflection   [rɪˈflɛkʃən]   *n.*   反對；水中映象

Narcissus fell for his own reflection.

納希瑟斯愛上他自己的倒影。

Narcissus，希臘少年，愛上自己在湖中的倒影，後憔悴而死，變成一株水仙。

25 again   [əˈgɛn]   *adv.*   再

Would you say that again?

請你再說一遍好嗎？

26 **planet**　[ˈplænɪt]　*n.*　行星

Mars is the fourth planet in order from the sun.

火星是太陽系的第四顆行星。

27 **voyage**　[ˈvɔɪɪdʒ]　*n.*　航海；航行

They went on a voyage last month.

他們上個月去航行。

We had a good voyage.

我們有了一趟愉快的航行。

go on a voyage 繼續航行

28 **luggage**　[ˈlʌgɪdʒ]　*n.*　行李；皮箱，皮包

They had left the luggage at the station.

他們將行李留在車站。

【同】baggage

29 **lose**　[luz]　*vt.*　失去；迷失；輸掉

He lost his life in the war.

他在戰爭中喪生。

lose one's way 迷路

lose the game 輸了比賽

30 **regain**　[rɪˈgen]　*vt.*　恢復，重回

When will the patient regain consciousness?

這個病人什麼時候恢復知覺？

主題 2
Place & Nature
地點與大自然

**Unit
01**

Home 家

Track 13

1　address　[əˋdrɛs]　*n.*　地址；演說；談吐

There isn't enough space for my address.

寫地址的地方不夠。

change one's address 變更地址

2　location　[loˋkeʃən]　*n.*　定位，測位；測量

We must decide on the location of our new store.

我們先得給新店舖選個地點。

3　habitation　[͵hæbəˋteʃən]　*n.*　居住，住所

This house is unfit for human habitation.

這房子不適合人居住。

4　house　[haʊs]　*n.*　房屋，住宅；商號

They built a house by the roadside.

他們在路邊蓋了一間房子。

keep house 管家

in front of the house 在房子的前面

5 **over** [`ovə] *prep.* 在…之上

We lived over a small cafe.

我們住在一家小咖啡館樓上。

6 **belong** [bə`lɔŋ] *vi.* 屬於，附屬

That dictionary belongs to me.

那本字典是屬於我的。

belong to 屬於

belong to sb. 屬於某人

主題 2

7 **interior** [ɪn`tɪrɪə] *n.* 部 *adj.* 部的

The architect laid out the interior of the building.

設計師設計了這座建築的內部格局。

【同】internal, inside

【反】exterior

8 **design** [dɪ`zaɪn] *vt.* 設計 *n.* 設計；圖樣

Architects design buildings.

建築師設計房子。

design a new house for sb. 為人設計新房子

be designed to test a new way 目的是實驗新方法

9 **decorate** [`dɛkəˌret] *vt.* 裝飾，裝潢，修飾

We decorated the house for Christmas.

我們裝飾房屋過耶誕節。

10 comfortable　[`kʌmfɚtəb!]　*adj.*　舒適的，自在的

A comfortable house is an Eden.

一個舒適的家是一個伊甸園。

Make yourself comfortable.

請不要客氣。

11 pleasant　[`plɛzənt]　*adj.*　令人愉快的

The walk was very pleasant.

那次散步很愉快。

I had a pleasant time.

我有過一段快樂的時光。

pleasant weather 令人愉快的天氣

12 attic　[`ætɪk]　*n.*　閣樓，頂樓

My mom stored boxes of clothes in the attic.

我媽媽在閣樓放著幾箱衣服。

13 roof　[ruf]　*n.*　屋頂；頂，頂部

Find someone to fix the roof.

找人來修屋頂。

the roof of a house 房子的屋頂

the roof of a building 建築物的頂部

14 rafter　[`ræftɚ]　*n.*　椽子

The big rafter is broken.

粗大的椽子壞了。

15 **door** [dor] *n.* 門

We'll meet you at the front door.
我們會在前門與你相見。
knock at the door 敲門

16 **window** [ˋwɪndo] *n.* 窗子，窗 ，窗口

He looked out of the window.
他向窗外看去。
window shopping 逛商店
open the window 開窗戶

17 **stair** [stɛr] *n.* （常用複數）樓梯

He ran down the stairs.
他跑下樓梯。
a stair 一階樓梯
a flight of stairs 一段樓梯

18 **floor** [flor] *n.* 地板；樓層

Sweep the floor. It's really dirty.
掃一下地板，它很髒。
on the floor 在地上
on the first floor 在一樓

19 **furnace** [ˋfɝnɪs] *n.* 爐子，熔爐；鼓風爐

Our furnace keeps the whole house warm.
我們的暖氣爐讓整棟房子很溫暖。

主題 2

20 heating　[ˋhitɪŋ]　*n.*　加熱，供暖

Make sure the central heating is off.

中央供暖設備一定要關掉。

21 hearth　[hɑrθ]　*n.*　壁爐地面；爐邊

We sat by the hearth and listen to the radio.

我們坐在壁爐邊聽廣播。

22 exterior　[ɪkˋstɪrɪɚ]　*adj.*　外部的；對外的

We are painting the exterior walls of the house.

我們正在給房子的外牆塗漆。

【同】outer

【反】interior

23 yard　[jɑrd]　*n.*　碼（英美長度單位）；庭院

I parked the car in the front yard.

我將汽車停在前院裡。

24 mower　[ˋmoɚ]　*n.*　割草的人，割草機

The boss decided to buy a new lawn mower.

老闆決定買一台新的割草機。

25 fence　[fɛns]　*n.*　柵欄

He built a fence around the garden.

他在花園周園築了籬笆。

Build a fence to keep the dog in.

建籬笆為了防止狗進來。

26 **garden** [ˋgɑrdn] *n.* 花園，菜園；公園

What a beautiful garden!

一個多麼漂亮的花園！

in the garden 在花園裡

27 **brick** [brɪk] *n.* 磚，磚塊；磚狀物

His new house was built by himself, brick by brick.

他的新房子是他自己一塊磚、一塊磚砌起來的。

28 **dwell** [dwɛl] *n.* 居住 *vi.* 凝思，細想

They dwelled in London for two years.

他們在倫敦住了兩年。

29 **rent** [rɛnt] *n.* 租金，租 *vi.* 出租

The rent is due at the end of each quarter.

繳納租金以每季度末為期限。

30 **tenant** [ˋtɛnənt] *n.* 承擔人，房客，佃戶

We need to find a new tenant.

我們必須找到一個新房客。

主題 2

Unit
02

Rooms 房間

Track 14

1　cellar　[`sɛlɚ]　*n.*　地窖，地下室

My father built a wine cellar.

我爸爸建了一個酒窖。

2　wall　[wɔl]　*n.*　牆，壁，圍牆，城牆

The castle walls are very thick.

城堡的牆很厚。

on the wall 在牆上（在表面上）

in the wall 在牆上（在牆裡的洞等中）

3　closet　[`klɑzɪt]　*n.*　壁櫥；小房間

My mom gave me her closet.

我媽媽把她的衣櫥送我。

4　private　[`praɪvɪt]　adj .私人的；私下的

I would like to have a private talk with you.

我希望和你私下談談。

5　dresser　[`drɛsɚ]　*n.*　化妝台，化妝師，碗櫃

He is a famous dresser.

他是一位有名的化妝師。

6 drawer　[`drɔɚ]　*n.*　抽屜

He found the money hidden away in a drawer.

他找到了藏在抽屜裡的錢。

in the top drawer 在最上面的抽屜裡

7 store　[stor]　*vt.*　存貯，儲藏

He stored food in his cupboard.

他把食品存放在碗櫥裡。

store food 儲藏食物

department store 百貨商店

主題 2

8 mess　[mɛs]　*n.*　混亂，混雜，骯髒

Would you please clean up the mess?

請你把這些骯髒的東西清理掉好嗎？

9 soap　[sop]　*n.*　肥皂

Wash your hands with soap.

用肥皂洗手。

a cake of soap 一塊肥皂

wash one's hands with soap 用肥皂洗手

10 bath　[bæθ]　*n.*　浴，洗澡；浴缸

I need to take a bath right away.

我需要馬上洗個澡。

take (have) a bath 洗澡

11 bathe [beð] *vt.* 給……洗澡；弄濕

Will you help me to bathe the baby?

孩子洗澡嗎？

bathe in the lake 在湖裡洗澡

go bathing in the river 去河裡洗澡

12 toilet [`tɔɪlɪt] *n.* 廁所，盥洗室，浴室

He wants to go to the toilet.

他想上廁所。

【同】lavatory, WC, loo, washroom

13 living room *n.* 起居室

What a lovely living room!

多麼可愛的起居室！

14 corridor [`kɔrɪdɚ] *n.* 走廊，回廊，通路

I met the boy whom I adore in the corridor.

我在走廊上遇到我喜歡的那個男孩。

【同】aisle, passage, porch

15 kitchen [`kɪtʃɪn] *n.* 廚房

My mother cleans the kitchen every day.

我媽媽每天打掃廚房。

get inside the kitchen 進去廚房

fall off the kitchen table 從廚房桌上掉下來

16 sink　　[sɪŋk]　*n.*　（廚房內的）水槽

Keep the sink clean.

保持水槽的清潔。

17 cupboard　　[ˋkʌbəd]　*n.*　碗櫃，碗碟櫥；櫥櫃

Harry Potter lived in the cupboard.

哈利波特住在碗櫥裡。

【同】cabinet, locker, closet

18 spoon　　[spun]　*n.*　匙，調羹

The little boy cannot find his favorite spoon.

那個小男孩找不到他最喜歡的湯匙。

a teaspoon 小茶匙

a silver spoon 銀匙

19 fork　　[fɔrk]　*n.*　叉；餐叉

Use a fork when having pasta.

吃義大利麵時用叉子。

the fork in the road 路的分叉

a knife and fork 一套刀叉

20 eat　　[it]　*vt.*　吃，喝　*vi.*　吃飯

Where shall we eat today?

今天我們去哪裡吃飯？

eat up 吃完，吃光

eat to live 為活吃

21 **bedroom**　[`bɛd,rʊm]　*n.*　臥室

When I was a little girl, I hoped I could have my own bedroom.

當我還是小女孩時，我希望有自己的房間。

22 **quilt**　[kwɪlt]　*n.*　被子

We don't have enough quilts for winter.

我們沒有足夠的被子過冬。

23 **sheet**　[ʃit]　*n.*　被單；紙張；薄板

Did you change the new sheet?

你換了新床單了嗎？

24 **crib**　[krɪb]　*n.*　嬰兒小床，食槽，柵欄

The baby was sleeping quietly in his crib.

嬰兒在他的小床裡靜靜地睡著。

【同】plagiarize

25 **closet**　[`klɑzɪt]　*n.*　壁櫥；小房間

Put the coats back into the closet.

請把大衣放回到壁櫥裡。

26 curtain　[`kɜtn]　*n.*　（窗、門）簾；幕

Draw the curtain, please.

請拉上窗簾。

Be quiet. The curtain rose.

安靜點，表演開始了。

draw the curtain back 拉上簾子

27 pillow　[`pɪlo]　*n.*　枕頭

Do you have an extra pillow?

你有多的枕頭嗎？

28 sofa　[`sofə]　*n.*　長沙發，沙發

She lay on the sofa, watching TV.

她躺在沙發上看電視。

29 cushion　[`kʊʃən]　*n.*　軟墊子

She bought cushions for her new home.

她為新家買了坐墊。

put one's head on a cushion 頭枕在墊子上

30 carpet　[`kɑrpɪt]　*n.*　毛毯；地毯

The cat slept on the carpet.

貓在地毯上睡覺。

a carpet of leaves 像地毯般的一層樹葉

主題 2

Restaurant 餐廳

Track 15

1 restaurant [ˋrɛstərənt] *n.* 餐館，飯店，菜館

We invited our new partner to dinner at an Italian restaurant.

我們邀請我們的新夥伴去一家義大利餐廳用餐。

2 counter [ˋkaʊntə] *n.* 櫃檯

He placed the money on the counter.

他把錢放在櫃檯上。

3 host [host] *n.* 主人；東道主

The host prepared lots of delicious dishes and wine for us.

主人為我們準備很多美味的菜餚和飲酒。

4 bill [bɪl] *n.* 帳單；招貼；票據

I can't pay now; please bill me later.

我現在不能付款，請以後開帳單給我。

a 100-dollar bill 一張一百元帳單

book bill 鈔票

5 reserve [rɪˋzɝv] *vt.* 儲備，保留；預定

Please reserve a room for me.

請為我預定一個房間。

6 **guest** [gɛst] *n.* 客人

These Japanese guests prefer to go shopping.

這些日本客人偏好逛街。

7 **napkin** [`næpkɪn] *n.* 餐巾（紙）

He handed me a napkin.

他遞給我一條餐巾。

8 **dish** [dɪʃ] *n.* 盤，碟；一道菜

My mom asked my brother to do the dishes.

我媽媽叫我弟弟去洗碗。

serve guests a dinner with dishes

服務客人與菜的晚餐

a dish of 一盤……

9 **plate** [plet] *n.* 盤子；碟子

She put the peaches on a plate.

她把桃子放在一個盤子裡。

eat two plates of 吃兩盤的…

10 **tray** [tre] *n.* 拖盤；淺盤；碟

She set a tray down on the table.

她把拖盤放在桌子上了。

11 **fancy** [`fænsɪ] *n.* 想像力；設想；愛好 *adj.* 精緻的

The poet has a lively fancy.

詩人想像力豐富。

12 **delicacy** [ˋdɛləkəsɪ] *n.* 細軟，精緻，精美的食品，嬌氣

He provided local delicacies for his guests' meal.

他用當地的美味佳餚來招待客人。

13 **simple** [ˋsɪmp!] *adj.* 單純的；簡易的

He has a simple heart.

他有一顆單純的心。

That question is very simple.

那個問題很簡單。

14 **bacon** [ˋbekən] *n.* 培根，燻豬肉

We had bacon and eggs for breakfast.

我們早餐吃培根和蛋。

15 **steak** [stek] *n.* 大塊牛肉；牛排

I've ordered a steak.

我要了一份牛排。

16 **cook** [kʊk] *vi.* 烹調，煮 *n.* 廚師

Carol often cooks for her family.

卡羅常常替她的家人做飯。

cook in the kitchen 在廚房裡做飯

home cooking 家常做法

17 **raw** [rɔ] *adj.* 未煮過的；未加工的

Most fruits are eaten raw.

大部分的水果是生吃的。

18 ingredient [ɪn`gridɪənt] *n.* 配料，成分

What are the ingredients of the cake?

這蛋糕是用哪些原料做成的？

【同】constituent

19 salt [sɔlt] *n.* 鹽

The fried chicken is too salty.

那炸雞太鹹了。

in the salt water 在鹽水裡

the Great Salt Lake 大鹽湖

20 pepper [`pɛpɚ] *n.* 胡椒，胡椒粉

The pepper in the food made me sneeze.

這食物中的胡椒味兒嗆得我直打噴嚏。

21 dessert [dɪ`zɝt] *n.* 甜點

We like to have cake for dessert after dinner.

我們喜歡在晚餐後吃蛋糕當甜點。

22 bar [bɑr] *n.* 酒吧間；條，杆；柵

There are several bars in the hotel.

這家旅館裡有好幾個酒吧。

23 birthday [`bɝθ,de] *n.* 生日

What's your plan on your girlfriend's birthday?

你女朋友生日那天有什麼計畫？

birthday party 生日聚會

24 banquet 　[`bæŋkwɪt]　*n.*　宴會，盛會，酒席

We had a good time at the banquet.

我們在宴會上度過一段好時光。

25 feast 　[fist]　*n.*　盛宴，筵席；節日

Christmas is an important feast for Christians.

耶誕節是基督教徒的一個重要節日。

26 pot 　[pɑt]　*n.*　罐；鍋；壺

She made a pot of tea for her guests.

她給客人沏了一壺茶。

a teapot 茶壺

coffee pot 咖啡壺

27 style 　[staɪl]　*n.*　風格；文體；式樣

The letter is written in a formal style.

這封信以正式文體寫成。

28 smoke 　[smok]　*n.*　煙；抽煙　*vi.*　冒煙

Do you smoke?

你抽煙嗎？

stop smoking 戒煙

have a smoke 抽根煙

29 **tip**　　[tɪp]　　*n.*　　小費；梢，尖端；提示

The artist painted in some very fine lines with the tip of a brush.

畫家用畫筆尖繪上了一些極細的線條。

I gave the waiter a tip.

我給了侍者小費。

reading tips 閱讀提示

30 **afford**　　[əˋford]　　*vt.*　　擔負得起⋯⋯；提供

These trees afford a pleasant shade.

這些樹提供了蔭涼。

afford to do sth. 付得起錢做某事

afford to pay sb. more money 能付得起某人更多

主題 2

Unit
04

Airport 機場

Track 16

1 tower [ˋtaʊɚ] *n.* 塔

There are lots of paintings in the tower.
塔中有很多幅畫。

The highest part of the church is its big, square tower.
教堂的最高部分是它的大方塔。

You can see the tower of the castle from here.
從這你能夠看到城堡的高塔。

2 portal [ˋport!] *n.* 入口，大門

The portal of the mansion is grand.
豪宅的大門很雄偉。

3 security [sɪˋkjʊrətɪ] *n.* 安全，安全感

The authorities have promised to review their security measurement.
當局已經答應重新檢查他們的安全措施。

4 gate [get] *n.* 大門

The gate is too narrow for a car.
車進不去。

meet outside the school gate 在校門外見面

go through the gate 穿過大門

5 expire　[ɪk`spaɪr]　*vi.*　滿期，到期；斷氣

My passport is due to expire in two months.

我的護照再過兩個月就到期了。

6 airport　[`ɛr,port]　*n.*　機場，航空站

The plane circled the airport before landing.

飛機在著陸之前在機場上空盤旋。

7 plane　[plen]　*n.*　平面；飛機

The quickest means of travel is by plane.

最快的交通工具是飛機。

8 pilot　[`paɪlət]　*n.*　領航員；飛行員

The pilot landed the plane safely.

駕駛員使飛機安全降落。

9 elevator　[`ɛlə,vetɚ]　*n.*　電梯；升降機

We took the elevator to the top floor.

我們搭電梯去頂樓。

【同】lift

10 descend　[dɪ`sɛnd]　*vi.*　下來，下降；下傾

We descend on foot after work.

我們下班後走路下樓。

11 **wing**　[wɪŋ]　*n.*　翅膀

The bird spread its wings.

那鳥伸展開它的翅膀。

flying wings 正在飛行的翅膀

12 **helicopter**　[ˋhɛlɪkɑptɚ]　*n.*　直升機

We took a helicopter to see the Great Barrier Reef.

我們搭直升機去看大堡礁。

13 **whirl**　[hwɝl]　*vt.*　*vi.*　*n.*　（使）旋轉

People whirled round the dancing floor.

人們在舞池裡旋轉。

14 **horizon**　[hәˋraɪzn]　*n.*　地平線；眼界，見識

The land loomed on the horizon.

陸地隱約浮現在地平線。

【同】skyline, scope, range

15 **passenger**　[ˋpæsndʒɚ]　*n.*　乘客；旅客

Passengers should fasten their seat belts.

乘客必須繫好安全帶。

There were few passengers on the bus.

公共汽車裡沒有幾個乘客。

the passengers of a ship 船上的旅客

16 check　[tʃɛk]　*n.*　支票

She wrote her friend a check.

她開了一張支票給她的朋友。

check in 報到，簽到，住飯店登記

check out 查明，結帳，查出

17 information　[ˌɪnfə`meʃən]　*n.*　消息，資訊；通知

Do you need any information about the corporation?

你需要任何公司的資料嗎？

the information on the computer 關於電腦的資訊

need some information about sb. 需要關於某人的資料

主題 2

18 assign　[ə`saɪn]　*vt.*　指派；分配；指定

Every student was assigned a project.

每位學生都分配到一項專題研究。

19 attach　[ə`tætʃ]　*vt.*　縛，系，貼；附加

My aunt attached a label to her baggage.

我的姑姑往行李上貼了一個標籤。

20 baggage　[`bægɪdʒ]　*n.*　行李

Her baggage has cleared customs.

她的行李已通過海關檢查。

21 aboard　[ə`bord]　*adv.*　上船（飛機、車）

All aboard!

請上船！

22 **flight** [flaɪt] *n.* 航班；飛行；逃跑

I book a direct flight to Paris.

我訂了直飛巴黎的班機。

make a round-the-world flight 做一個環遊世界飛行

the flight of time 光陰飛逝

23 **attendant** [əˋtɛndənt] *n.* 侍者；護理人員

He is an attendant in this hotel.

他是這家飯店的侍者。

24 **landing** [ˋlændɪŋ] *n.* 上岸，登陸，著陸

Happy landing.

祝你平安著陸。

25 **trolley** [ˋtrɑlɪ] *n.* 手推車；無軌電車

We need a trolley, or we are unable to move these heavy boxes.

我們需要一輛手推車，否則我們無法搬動這些沉重的箱子。

26 **transport** [ˋtræns͵pɔrt] *n.* 運輸；運輸工具

How is the public transport in this city?

這座城市的大眾交通運輸如何？

It took all day to transport the furniture to the new building.

我花了整天的時間把家具運送到新大樓去。

You can transport goods from one place to another by train or bus.

你可以用火車或公車運送貨物到從一個地方另一個地方 。

27 rapid　[ˋræpɪd]　*adj.*　快的，迅速的

She is making rapid progress in her work.

她在工作上進步突飛猛進。

a rapid stream 急流

a rapid train 快車

28 transportation　[ˌtrænspɚˋteʃən]　*n.*　運輸，運送，客運

The elderly can have free transportation if they apply for the identification card.

老人如果申請識別證，就可以免費搭乘交通運輸工具。

主題 2

29 cab　[kæb]　*n.*　計程車

Get a cab. Don't walk home at night.

搭計程車吧。晚上別走路回家。

【同】taxi

30 van　[væn]　*n.*　大篷車，運貨車；休旅車

The van will take you to the airport from downtown.

休旅車將帶您從市中心到機場。

Unit
05

City 城市

Track 17

1 lure [lʊr] *n.* 誘惑力，引誘

No one can resist the lure of chocolate.

沒有人可以抵抗巧克力的誘惑。

【同】entice, tempt, enchant

2 swell [swɛl] *vi. vt.* 使膨脹，隆起

There was a swell in the city's population.

該市出現人口膨脹。

3 million [ˋmɪljən] *n.* 百萬；百萬個

There are four million residents in the city.

這個城市有四百萬個居民。

millions of 數以百萬計的

millions more people 百萬多人

4 mass [mæs] *n.* （聚成一體的）團，塊；一群

There was a mass of flowers in the garden.

院子裡有一叢花。

masses of people 一大群人

a mass of flowers 一叢花

5　noise　　[nɔɪz]　　*n.*　　喧鬧聲；響聲；雜訊

It is impolite to make any noise at midnight.

半夜製造噪音是不禮貌的。

No noise, please.

請安靜。

make a noise 喧鬧

6　crime　　[kraɪm]　　*n.*　　罪，罪行；犯罪

Whoever commits a crime should be punished.

犯罪的人應該被懲罰。

主題 2

7　robbery　　[ˋrɑbərɪ]　　*n.*　　搶劫，劫掠，盜取

A bank robbery has happened recently in the capital city.

首都最近發生一件銀行搶劫案。

8　expansion　　[ɪkˋspænʃən]　　*n.*　　擴大，擴充；擴張

The suburbs are an expansion of cities.

郊區是城市的延伸。

9　undergo　　[͵ʌndəˋgo]　　*vt.*　　經歷，經受，忍受

The country underwent great change.

這個國家經歷了巨大的變化。

【同】experience, suffer, sustain

10　borough　　[ˋbɝo]　　*n.*　　享有自治權的市鎮或區

Brooklyn is one of the five boroughs of New York City.

布魯克林區是紐約市的五個行政區之一。

11 **building** [ˋbɪldɪŋ] *n.* 建築物，大樓；建築

The World Trade Center in New York City was one of the world's tallest buildings.

紐約的世界貿易中心曾是世界上最高的建築物之一。

classroom building 教學樓

12 **sidewalk** [ˋsaɪd͵wɔk] *n.* 人行道

He paced on the sidewalk.

他在人行道上踱步。

13 **street** [strit] *n.* 街道

I met him in the street.

我在街上遇到他。

on the street 在街上（美國用法）

in the street 在街上（英國用法）

14 **light** [laɪt] *n.* 光 *adj.* 明亮的

It's beginning to get light.

天漸漸亮了。

traffic light 交通指示燈

light blue 淺藍色的

15 **conspicuous** [kənˋspɪkjʊəs] *adj.* 顯著的，顯而易見的

You must wear conspicuous clothes on rainy days in case drivers can't notice you.

你下雨天出門一定要穿顯眼的衣服，以防駕駛無法注意到你。

【同】obvious, noticeable

16 avenue　[ˋævəˌnju]　*n.*　林蔭道，道路；大街

Books are avenues to knowledge.

書是通向知識的道路。

17 alley　[ˋælɪ]　*n.*　小巷，小徑

There is a narrow alley at the end of the street.

街道的盡頭有一條狹窄的小巷。

18 road　[rod]　*n.*　路，道路，公路

The road was blocked by a huge rock.

道路被一塊大石頭堵住了。

along the road 沿著這條路

by the side of the road 靠路邊

19 route　[rut]　*n.*　路；路線

The route is quite complicated.

路線很複雜。

20 chaos　[ˋkeɑs]　*n.*　混亂

The classroom is in chaos.

教室一團混亂。

【同】disorder, confusion, moil

【反】order, regularity

21 shop　[ʃɑp]　*n.*　商店，店鋪；車間

I usually go shopping on Sundays.

我通常星期天購物。

22 grocery　［`grosərı］　n.　食品雜貨店

He inherited his father's grocery store.

他繼承他父親的雜貨店。

23 supermarket　［`supəˌmarkıt］　n.　超級市場

The housewife goes to supermarket once a week.

家庭主婦一個禮拜去超級市場一次。

24 clothing　［`kloðıŋ］　n.　衣服，被褥

This clothing sells well to the office lady market.

這種衣服在上班族女郎之間很暢銷。

25 fashionable　［`fæʃənəb!］　adj.　流行的，時髦的

She is a fashionable woman.

她是一個時髦的女人。

26 concert　［`kansət］　n.　音樂會；演奏會

I've bought the ticket to the concert.

我已經買了音樂會的票。

27 train　［tren］　n.　火車

She decides to take the train to go home.

她決定搭火車回家。

get on the train 上火車

get off the train 下火車

28 ride [raɪd] *vt.* *vi.* 騎（馬，自行車）

He rides a bicycle to school.

他騎腳踏車上學。

ride on a bus 搭巴士，乘公共汽車

ride on a train 乘火車前往

29 reside [rɪˋzaɪd] *vi.* 居住，駐紮；屬於

We resided in the hotel on our honeymoon.

我們蜜月時住在飯店。

30 guard [gɑrd] *n.* 哨兵，警衛員

Find the guard immediately.

馬上找警衛來。

guard against 防止，避免

put a guard round the pool 在水池的周圍放個護欄

Country 鄉下

 Track 18

1 farm [farm] *n.* 農場

We work on the farm.

我們在農場工作。

on the farm 在農場上

deer farm 鹿場

2 farmyard [`farm,jard] *n.* 農家庭院

There is a tractor in this farmyard.

在這個農家庭院裡停著一台牽引機。

farmhand 農場工人

farmhouse 農舍

3 barn [barn] *n.* 穀倉；糧倉

The old lady owns a barn.

老婦人擁有一座穀倉。

4 brand [brænd] *n.* 商品；烙印　　*vt.* 銘刻

The brand of shoes is her favorite.

這個牌子的鞋子是她的最愛。

5 manure　　[mə`njʊr]　*n.*　　肥料，糞肥

Animal dung may be used as manure.

動物的糞便可以作為肥料使用。

6 trough　　[trɔf]　*n.*　　木缽，水槽，馬槽

I can't find my horse at the trough.

我在馬槽邊找不到我的馬。

7 mud　　[mʌd]　*n.*　　軟泥，泥漿

He removed the mud from his shoes.

他去掉鞋上的泥。

Oh-no! My new shoes are covered with mud.

喔不！我的新鞋沾滿了泥巴。

8 cemetery　　[`sɛmə,tɛrɪ]　*n.*　　公墓；墓地

He visited his wife's grave in the cemetery every week.

他每週都去掃他太太的墓。

【同】graveyard

9 orchard　　[`ɔrtʃəd]　*n.*　　果園

She ran hither and thither in the orchard.

她在果園裡到處跑。

10 residence　　[`rɛzədəns]　*n.*　　居住；駐紮；住處

Residence in the area qualifies you for membership.

只要在本區居住就可入會。

主題 2

11 **neighbor** [ˋnebɚ] *n.* 鄰居

My neighbor is a friendly old lady.
我的鄰居是個友善的老婦人。

12 **lane** [len] *n.* （鄉間）小路；跑道

We often walked down this lane to school when we were little.
我們小時候常常走這條路去上學。

13 **gravel** [ˋgrævl] *n.* 砂礫；砂礫層；結石

The kid is playing on the road covered with gravel.
小孩在用礫石鋪成的路上玩。
【同】pebble

14 **pathway** [ˋpæθ͵we] *n.* 路，徑

It is a difficult pathway to success.
成功是一條艱難的路。

The pathway was rough and covered with little stones.
這條路高低不平，鋪滿了小石頭。

15 **irrigation** [͵ɪrəˋgeʃən] *n.* 灌溉；沖洗法

We need to set up an irrigation project.
我們必須興建灌溉工程了。
irrigate *vt.* 灌溉

16 grain　　[gren]　　*n.*　　穀物，谷類；谷粒

They ship grain to Latin America.

他們把穀物運往拉丁美洲。

grain imports 糧食進口

a grain of sand 一粒沙子

17 crop　　[krɑp]　　*n.*　　莊稼；收成

The farmer hired two men to gather the crops.

農場主雇了兩名工人收割莊稼。

main crops 主要的那些農作物

a good crop of potatoes 馬鈴薯豐收

18 cultivate　　[`kʌltə,vet]　　*vt.*　　耕；種植；培養

Only one third of the land can be cultivated.

只有三分之一的土地可以耕種。

19 plow　　[plaʊ]　　*n.*　　犁　*vt.*　　*vi.*　　犁，耕

Farmers now use tractors to plow their fields.

現今農民用牽引機耕地。

20 mow　　[mo]　　*n.*　　草堆，皺眉；刈（草坪等）上的草

Early sow, early mow.

【諺】早種早收。

主題 2

21 **field**　[fild]　*n.*　地，田地

They were working in the cotton fields.

他們在棉田裡幹活。

in the field 在地裡

field trip 野外旅遊

22 **weed**　[wid]　*n.*　雜草，野草　*vi.*　除草

The garden is choked with weeds.

花園雜草叢生。

23 **district**　[ˋdɪstrɪkt]　*n.*　區，行政區；地區

There is a shopping district in this suburb.

這個郊區有一個商圈。

the Northeast district 東北地區

a police district 員警管區

24 **land**　[lænd]　*n.*　陸地

Most mammals live on land.

大多數哺乳動物生活在陸地上。

by land 由陸路

rich land 肥沃的土地

25 **space**　[spes]　*n.*　空間；場地；空白

The sofa takes up a lot of space in the living room.

這張沙發佔了客廳很大的空間。

space ship 太空船

space station 太空站

26 breadth [brɛdθ] *n.* 寬度，幅度；幅面

The area can easily be worked out if you know the length and the breadth.

如果你知道長度和寬度的話，計算面積就很容易了。

27 area [ˋɛrɪə] *n.* 地區

Dogs are not allowed in this area.

禁止將狗帶入這個區域。

hit this area 襲擊這個地區

from area to area 從一個地區到一個地區

28 rural [ˋrʊrəl] *adj.* 農村的，田園的

The disease occurs frequently in rural areas.

那疾病多見於農村地區。

29 village [ˋvɪlɪdʒ] *n.* 鄉村，村莊

The village is as beautiful as a wonderland.

這個村莊美如仙境。

in the village 在村子裡

a fishing village 漁村

30 picturesque [ˌpɪktʃəˋrɛsk] *adj.* 生動的，如畫的，獨特的

The poet lived in a picturesque village.

這個詩人住在風景如畫的村莊裡。

a picturesque village 風景如畫的村莊

Unit
07

Ocean 海洋

 Track 19

1　sea　[si]　*n.*　海洋，海

Children like to go swimming in the sea.
小孩喜歡去海裡游泳。

2　bay　[be]　*n.*　海灣

The ship sailed into a secluded bay.
船駛進一個僻靜的海灣。

3　explore　[ɪk`splor]　*vt.*　*vi.*　探險，探索

The students have explored the issues since last semester.
學生們上學期就在探討這個議題了。

4　biology　[baɪ`ɑlədʒɪ]　*n.*　生物學；生態學

He specializes in biology.
他主修生物學。

5　water　[`wɔtə]　*n.*　水

Fish live in water.
魚生活在水中。
water pollution 水污染
on the water 在水上

118

6　drift　[drɪft]　*vi.*　漂流，漂泊　*n.*　漂流

A boat drifted slowly downstream.

一艘船緩緩地往下游漂去。

7　multitude　[`mʌltə,tjud]　*n.*　大批，大群；大量

The development of public transportation satisfies the
needs of the multitudes.

交通運輸的發展滿足了大眾的需求。

主題 2

8　river　[`rɪvə]　*n.*　江，河

She visited the River Seine last month.

她上個月造訪了塞納河。

in the river 在河裡

the River Thames 泰晤士河

9　swim　[swɪm]　*vi.*　游，游泳；眼花

Let's go swimming.

咱們游泳去。

10　whale　[hwel]　*n.*　鯨；龐然大物

The residents of the town found a whale carcass by the
beach.

城鎮的居民在海灘邊發現一隻鯨魚的屍體。

11　turtle　[`tɜt!]　*n.*　海龜，玳瑁；甲魚肉

The little boy keeps a fresh-water turtle.

小男孩養了一隻淡水龜。

12 **beach** [bitʃ] *n.* 海灘，湖灘，河灘

We are basking on the beach.

我們在海灘上曬太陽。

on the beach 在海濱

a beach umbrella 海水浴用的遮陽傘

13 **barefoot** [ˋbɛr,fʊt] *adv.* *adj.* 赤腳（的）

We walked around the beach barefoot.

我們赤著腳在海灘上走來走去。

14 **ship** [ʃɪp] *n.* 輪船

That ship was due to sail the following morning but canceled.

那艘船定於第二天啟航，但取消了。

15 **captain** [ˋkæptɪn] *n.* 陸軍上尉；隊長

Richard is the captain of the football team.

理查德是這個橄欖球隊的隊長。

the captain of a ship 船長

16 **vessel** [ˋvɛs!] *n.* 容器；船，飛船；管

We hove the vessel to.

我們把船停住了。

17 **tide** [taɪd] *n.* 潮；潮水

Watch out! The tide is in.

小心！潮水漲了。

18 tempestuous [tɛmˈpɛstʃʊəs] *adj.* 狂暴的

They finally divorced after a tempestuous marriage.

經歷一段狂風暴雨似的婚姻後，他們終於離婚了。

19 dive [daɪv] *n.* 跳水；潛水；俯衝

What a beautiful dive!

多麼優美的跳水！

dive to 潛到

dive down to the bottom 潛到底部

主題 2

20 coral [ˈkɔrəl] *n.* 珊瑚

Coral is formed by certain types of polyp.

珊瑚是由某些水螅體構成的。

21 fin [fɪn] *n.* 鰭

The fish's dorsal fin was hurt.

這條魚的背鰭受傷了。

22 gill [gɪl] *n.* 鰓

Gills are the organ through which fish breathe.

鰓是魚類用來呼吸的器官。

23 **float** [flot] *vi.* 漂浮 *vt.* 使漂浮

An empty glass bottle floats on the sea.

玻璃空瓶子在海上漂浮。

I saw wood float on water.

我看到木頭漂浮在水上。

Dust floats in the air.

塵土漂浮在空氣中。

24 **island** [drɪft] *n.* 島

There are many islands in the sea.

海中有很多島嶼。

Can you see the small island in the middle of the lake?

你有看見湖中有一座小島嗎？

25 **surround** [səˋraʊnd] *vt.* 環繞，圈住，圍

The police surrounded the house.

員警包圍了這幢房子。

26 **discover** [dɪsˋkʌvɚ] *vt.* 發現；暴露，顯示

She discovered the joy of singing.

她感到了唱歌的樂趣。

Who discovered America in 1492?

誰在 1492 年發現了美洲？

discover that... 發現…

27 marine　[məˋrin]　*adj.*　海的；海上的

We went to the marine museum last week.

我們上禮拜去海事博物館。

28 type　[taɪp]　*n.*　類型；樣式

What type of house would you prefer to live in?

你喜愛住哪一類房子？

different types of 各種形式的

all types of 各種形式的

主題 2

29 bottom　[ˋbɑtəm]　*n.*　底，底部，根基

The bottom of the cup is broken.

這杯子的底破了。

at the bottom of 在底部

go to the bottom of 到…的底部

30 feeder　[ˋfidɚ]　*n.*　飼養者，供給者，奶瓶

The baby is a noisy feeder.

這個小嬰孩吃東西時發出聲響。

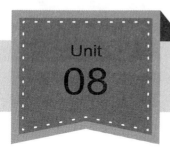

Woods 森林

Track 20

1 hill   [hɪl]   *n.*   小山

There is a red house that stands on the hill.

山丘上有一座紅房子。

on the hill 在山上

move into the hills 搬到山裡

2 tree   [tri]   *n.*   樹

He planted a tree in the yard.

他在庭院種一棵樹。

in the tree 在樹上（待在樹上）

on the tree 在樹上（果實等長在樹上）

3 forest   [ˋfɔrɪst]   *n.*   森林

This is an oak forest.

這是個橡樹林。

be lost in the forest 在森林中迷路

go off into the forest 去到森林裡

4 timber   [ˋtɪmbɚ]   *n.*   木料；木材

The mansion is built of timber.

這棟宅邸由木材建成。

【同】wood, trees, forest, beam

5 **soil**　[sɔɪl]　*n.*　土壤；土地

Fertile soil yields good crops.

肥沃的土地能種出好莊稼。

stop the soil getting too dry 阻止土壤變得太乾

hold the soil in place 保持那個地方的土壤

6 **fern**　[fɝn]　*n.*　羊齒植物，蕨

There are many different types of ferns in her backyard.

她的後院裡長了多種羊齒植物。

7 **flower**　[`flaʊɚ]　*n.*　花，花卉；開花

The roses have been in flower for a week.

這些玫瑰花已經開了一星期了。

come into flower 開花

flowerbed 花壇

8 **fossil**　[`fɑsl̩]　*n.*　化石　*adj.*　化石的

He spent many years digging fossils.

他花費多年挖掘化石。

9 **deer**　[dɪr]　*n.*　鹿

Look out! A herd of deer is walking across the road.

小心！有一群鹿在過馬路。

主題 2

10 **bear** [bɛr] *n.* 熊；粗魯的人

I can't bear to see you like this.

我不忍見你這樣。

a polar bear 北極熊

11 **squirrel** [ˈskwɝəl] *n.* 松鼠

A squirrel hoards nuts for the winter.

松鼠為過冬貯藏堅果。

12 **nut** [nʌt] *n.* 堅果，乾果；螺母

Cashews and walnuts are both nuts.

腰果和核桃都是堅果。

13 **trail** [trel] *n.* 痕跡；小徑

The hounds found the trail of the rabbit.

獵犬發現了野兔的蹤跡。

14 **stroll** [strol] *n.* *vi.* 漫步；閒逛

We strolled along the beach after dinner.

我們晚餐後在海邊散步。

【同】saunter, amble, ramble, walk

15 **rest** [rɛst] *vi.* *vt.* （使）支撐（在）

Rest the ladder against the wall.

把梯子靠在牆上吧。

take a rest 休息

the rest rooms 廁所

16 outdoors [ˋaʊtˋdorz] *adv.* 在戶外，在野外

My sister and I often played outdoors when we were little.

我和我妹妹小時候常常在戶外玩耍。

17 tent [tɛnt] *n.* 帳篷

The boys put up their tent quickly.

男孩們很快地搭起他們的帳篷。

They pitched a tent by the stream.

他們在河邊搭了帳篷。

主題 2

18 hunt [hʌnt] *vi.* 打獵

November is a good time to hunt deer.

十一月正是獵鹿的好時節。

19 kill [kɪl] *vt.* 殺死

His wife was killed in a car accident.

他的妻子在車禍中喪生。

kill oneself 自殺

be killed in the accident 在意外事件中死亡

20 meat [mit] *n.* 肉

The cheap buyer takes bad meat.

【諺】便宜無好貨。

eat meat 吃肉

21 **snow**　　[sno]　*n.*　雪　*vi.*　下雪

It was snowing heavily.

天正在下大雪。

snow hard 下大雪

22 **Christmas**　　[`krɪsməs]　*n.*　耶誕節

Merry Christmas and a Happy New Year!

恭祝聖誕，並賀新禧！

Christmas trees 聖誕樹

Christmas cards 聖誕卡

23 **sled**　　[slɛd]　*n.*　雪橇，小雪橇

The husky is one kind of sled dog.

哈士奇是一種雪橇犬。

24 **cold**　　[kold]　*adj.*　冷的；冷淡的　*n.*　冷

It was bitterly cold that night.

那個夜晚，天氣十分寒冷。

catch a cold 感冒

take a cold 著涼，傷風

25 **sunrise**　　[`sʌn،raɪz]　*n.*　日出

I enjoy watching the sunrise in the mountains.

我喜歡在山上看日出。

26 beyond [bɪˋjɑnd] *prep.* 在⋯的那邊

Beyond the river is a forest.

河那邊是一片森林。

beyond belief 難以置信

beyond the reach of 為⋯力量（能力）所不能及

27 edge [ɛdʒ] *n.* 邊緣；邊

The couple built their house on the edge of the forest.

這對夫妻把他們的房子建在森林邊緣。

on the edge of the river 在河邊

on the edge of the mountain 在山邊

28 encamp [ɪnˋkæmp] *vi.* 紮營，露營

The army encamped in the forest for the night.

軍隊在森林中紮營過夜。

29 dusky [ˋdʌskɪ] *adj.* 微暗的，暗淡的；陰暗的

The maple leaves turn dusky red in autumn.

楓葉在秋天轉為暗紅。

30 sunset [ˋsʌn͵sɛt] *n.* 日落

The sunset here is very beautiful.

這裡的日落景色極美。

from sunrise to sunset 從日出到日落

主題 2

Unit
09

Weather 天氣

Track 21

1 weather [ˋwɛðɚ] *n.* 天氣

What's the weather like?
天氣怎麼樣？
weather station 氣象站
weather forecast 天氣預報

2 atmosphere [ˋætməs͵fɪr] *n.* 大氣；空氣；氣氛

The people are in a festive atmosphere.
各人們民都沉浸在節日的氣氛之中。
【同】air

3 shower [ˋʃaʊɚ] *vi.* 下陣雨　*vt.* 使濕透

I got caught in the shower on my way to school.
我在上學途中遇到那場雨。

4 thunder [ˋθʌndɚ] *n.* 雷　*vi.* 打雷　*vt.* 吼出

My sister is afraid of thunder.
我妹妹害怕雷聲。

5 lightning [ˋlaɪtnɪŋ] *n.* 閃電，閃電放電

The dark room was lit up by lightning.

黑暗的房間被閃電照亮。

6 strike [straɪk] *vt.* *vi.* 打；擊

He was struck by lightning.

他被閃電擊中。

He struck me on the head.

他打我的頭。

strike a match for a cigarette 劃一根火柴點煙

7 thunderbolt [ˋθʌndə,bolt] *n.* 霹靂，雷電；意外；怒喝

The news of his decease came up his son like a thunderbolt.

他過世的消息對他兒子來說簡直晴天霹靂。

8 heavy [ˋhɛvɪ] *adj.* 重的

She left the studio with a heavy heart.

她懷著沉重的心情離開工作室。

have a heavy rainfall 下了一場大雨

9 heat [hit] *n.* 熱，炎熱 *vi.* 變熱

The stove heats the room.

暖爐使房間溫暖起來。

The sun heated the earth.

太陽使地球暖和。

work in this heat 在熱的天氣裡工作

10 **temperature** [ˋtɛmprətʃɚ] *n.* 溫度

The doctor took her temperature and gave her a prescription.

醫生測量她的體溫，並開處方箋。

11 **frost** [frɑst] *n.* 冰凍，嚴寒；霜

The frost killed the young plants.

寒霜凍死了幼苗。

12 **icy** [ˋaɪsɪ] *adj.* 冰冷的；冷冰冰的

I was hit by an icy blast of air when I opened the door this morning.

今天早上我打開門時，一陣刺骨的寒風便向我襲來。

【同】cold, chilly, stony

【反】hot

13 **snowy** [snoɪ] *adj.* 雪的，下雪的

Kids are looking forward to a snowy winter.

孩子們期盼下雪的冬天。

14 **sift** [sɪft] *vt.* 篩，過濾 *vi.* 通過

A diamond is sifted from sand.

鑽石從沙裡淘出來。

【同】filter, sieve, sort

15 **cover** [ˋkʌvɚ] *vt.* 蓋，包括 *n.* 蓋子

The highway was covered with snow.

公路被雪覆蓋著。

cover sth. with sth. 用某東西蓋某東西
cover the event 報導那個事件

16 melt　[mɛlt]　*vi.*　融化　*vt.*　使融化

The sun melted the snow.
太陽使雪融化。

17 ray　[re]　*n.*　光線，射線，輻射線

A ray of sunshine shone through the clouds.
一縷陽光透過雲層。
a flaming ray 光焰般的光輝
give off rays 發出光線

18 sunny　[`sʌnɪ]　*adj.*　晴朗的

A high over southern Europe is bringing fine, sunny weather
to all parts of the continent.
歐洲南部上空的反氣旋給各地區帶來了晴朗的好天氣。
a sunny room 向陽的房間
a sunny smile 愉快的微笑

19 delightful　[dɪ`laɪtfəl]　*adj.*　令人愉快的，可喜的

She owns a delightful cottage.
她擁有一幢可愛的小木屋。

20 cloudy　[`klaʊdɪ]　*adj.*　多雲的，陰天的

Tonight will be cloudy.
今天夜間多雲。

21 dark [dɑrk] *adj.* 黑暗的

It's getting dark. Let's go home.

天色暗了，我們回家吧。

in the dark 在黑暗中

dark blue 深藍色

22 cool [kul] *vi. vt.* （使）涼快，冷卻

The hall is nice and cool.

大廳既漂亮又涼爽。

keep cool 保持冷靜

cool the beer 使啤酒冰涼

23 wind [wɪnd] *n.* 風

There is a hard wind blowing.

強風勁吹。

strong winds 大風

24 windy [ˋwɪndɪ] *adj.* 有風的；風大的

It's been windy all morning.

整個早上都有風。

25 blow [blo] *vt. vi.* 吹

The wind blew her hair.

風吹動她的頭髮。

blow off 吹掉

blow out 吹熄

26 toss　[tɔs]　*vi.*　翻來覆去

My husband was tossing and turning all night.

我丈夫整夜翻來覆去睡不著。

27 rainfall　[`ren,fɔl]　*n.*　降雨，降雨量

What is the average annual rainfall in this region?

這個地區的年平均降雨量是多少？

28 flood　[flʌd]　*n.*　洪水　*vt.*　淹沒

On Monday morning, we received a flood of emails.

星期一早上，我們收到如洪水般湧至的電子信件。

floods and floods of people 人山人海

a flooded street 一條洪水淹沒的街道

29 ensue　[ɛn`su]　*vi.*　跟著發生，繼起

After the lightning, thunder ensued.

閃電之後，雷聲至。

【同】follow

30 weary　[`wɪrɪ]　*adj.*　疲倦的　*vt.*　使疲乏

She is gradually weary of the work.

她漸漸地對工作感到厭倦。

主題 2

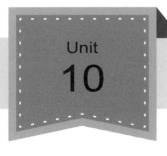

Color & Shape
顏色 & 形狀

 Track 22

1 yellow [ˋjɛlo] *adj.* 色的

She wore a yellow scarf.
她戴著黃色的圍巾。
Yellow River 河
the Yellow Sea 海

2 purple [ˋpɝpḷ] *n.* 紫色 *adj.* 紫的

She was dressed in purple.
她穿著紫色的衣服。

3 wave [wev] *n.* 波，波浪；波動

Her hair waves naturally.
她的頭髮自然鬈曲。
wave one's hand 揮手
wave one's hands 揮手（多人）

4 length [lɛŋθ] *n.* 長，長度；一段

The length of the concert is 3 hours.
音樂會長三小時。
10 meters in length 10 米長
at length 最終，終於

主題 2

5 width　[wɪdθ]　*n.*　寬闊，廣闊；寬度

She has a width of experience.

她有豐富的閱歷。

6 shape　[ʃep]　*n.*　形狀；情況　*vt.*　形成

This island is triangular in shape.

這個島的外形呈三角形。

7 define　[dɪˋfaɪn]　*vt.*　給…下定義；限定

The powers of a judge are defined by law.

法官的許可權是由法律規定的。

8 triangle　[ˋtraɪˌæŋg!]　*n.*　三角（形）

He outlined the triangle in red.

他用紅筆劃出三角形。

9 three　[θri]　*n.*　三

This chair has only three legs.

這把椅子只有三條腿。

come at three 在三點鐘來

three o'clock 三點鐘

10 line　[laɪn]　*vt.*　沿…排列　*vi.*　排隊

There is a long line at the ticket office.

售票處排著長長的隊伍。

wait in line 排隊等候

information line 資訊熱線

11 **point** [pɔɪnt] *n.* 觀點；論點；要點

I don't see the point of your paper.

我不明白你論文的觀點。

be on the point of doing sth. 正要做某事

be on the point 得到要領，中肯

12 **curve** [kɜv] *n.* 曲線；彎 *vt.* 弄彎

The path curves to the east.

這條小徑向右彎。

13 **circle** [ˋsɜk!] *vt.* 環繞，盤旋 *n.* 圓

Please circle the correct answers.

請圈出正確的答案。

a reading circle 讀書界

the family circle 家族

14 **green** [grin] *adj.* 綠色的

She never wears green.

她從不穿綠色的衣服。

green house 溫室

light green 淺綠色

15 **globe** [glob] *n.* 球；球狀物；地球

We use a globe in our geography lessons.

我們在地理課上用地球儀。

He sailed around the globe.

他環繞地球航行。

16 revolve [rɪˋvɑlv] *vt.* *vi.* （使）旋轉

A small motor makes the wheels revolve.

一台小馬達驅動著輪子旋轉。

【同】rotate, turn, spin, whirl

17 cube [kjub] *n.* 立方形；立方

A cube is a solid.

正方體是立體圖形。

18 rectangle [rɛkˋtæŋgl] *n.* 矩形，長方形

She folded the paper into a rectangle.

她把紙折成長方形。

having the shape of a rectangle 矩形的，具有矩形形狀的

19 four [for] *n.* 四

There are four wheels on a car.

一輛汽車有四個輪子。

at four 四點鐘

be four (years old) 四歲

20 angle [ˋæŋgl] *n.* 角，角度

I would like to know your angle in this discussion.

我想知道你對這項討論的觀點。

主題 2

21 **straight** [stret] *adj.* 直的；正直的 *adv.* 直

My little brother drew a circle and a straight line on the paper.

我的小弟弟在紙上畫了一個圈和一條直線。

a straight line 一條直線

go straight ahead 一直向前走

22 **pattern** [`pætɚn] *n.* 型，式樣，模，模型

Her dress has a flower pattern.

她的衣服有花的圖樣。

a pattern wife 理想的妻子

23 **repeat** [rɪ`pit] *vt.* 重說，重做 *n.* 重複

Please repeat what I said.

請重複我說的話。

repeat sth. to sb. 向某人重複某事

24 **change** [tʃendʒ] *n.* 零錢；找頭 *vt.* 兌換

Can you change a five-pound note?

你能換開五英鎊的票子嗎？

change... into... …變成…，…兌換…

be changed back into 被轉回去成為

25 **physical** [`fɪzɪk!] *adj.* 物理的

These are physical changes, while those are chemical changes.

這些是物理變化，而那些是化學變化。

26 **transform** [træns`fɔrm] *vt.* 改變；改造；變換

Power and wealth transformed his character and attitude entirely.

權力與財富完全改變了他的個性和態度。

【同】change, alter, adapt

【反】retain

27 **appearance** [ə`pɪrəns] *n.* 出現，來到；外觀

The singer made a television appearance.

這位歌手在電視上亮相。

28 **similar** [`sɪmələ-] *adj.* 相似的，類似的

These two buildings are similar on the whole.

從整體來看，這兩幢樓是相似的。

29 **opposite** [`ɑpəzɪt] *adj.* 對面的；相對的

We are completely opposite to each other in personality.

我們兩個人的個性天差地別。

move in the opposite direction 向相反方向移動

opposite the gate 在大門的對面

30 **outline** [`aʊt,laɪn] *n.* 輪廓；略圖；大綱

The professor asked us to give an outline for our report.

教授要求我們給我們的報告一個大綱。

Habitats 棲息地

Track 23

1 vast [væst] *adj.* 巨大的；大量的

She has saved a vast amount of money.
她已經存了一筆鉅款。

He spent a vast sum of money.
他花了一大筆錢。

The Sahara is a vast desert.
撒哈拉是一個大沙漠。

2 harsh [hɑrʃ] *adj.* 粗糙的；嚴厲的

He suddenly threw in a harsh word.
他突然插了一句嚴厲的話。

【同】severe, strict

【反】mild

3 dirt [dɝt] *n.* 塵，土；汙物，污垢

Wash the dirt off your hands.
把你手上的泥汙洗掉。

wash the dirt off the car 洗掉車上的髒物

4 sand　　[sænd]　*n.*　　沙，沙地

Hurry up! The sands of time are running out!

快點！時間不多了！

play on the sands 在沙灘上玩

on the sand 在沙地上，在沙子上

5 plain　　[plen]　*n.*　平原　*adj.*　　清楚的

It is plain that he is the boss.

很明顯，他是老闆。

His voice was clear and plain.

他的聲音清晰明白。

on the American plains 在美洲大平原上

主題 2

6 spacious　　[`speʃəs]　*adj.*　　廣闊的，廣大的

They have a spacious living room.

他們有一個寬敞的起居室。

【同】roomy, capacious, ample

7 dry　　[draɪ]　*vt.*　使乾　*vi.*　變乾

The well had gone dry.

井乾涸了。

dry air 乾燥的空氣

dry weather 不下雨的天氣

8 habitat　　[hɜd]　*n.*　產地；棲息地

The icy wastes of the Arctic are the polar bear's habitat.

北極圈所消耗的冰是北極熊的棲息地。

9 buffalo [ˋbʌf!ˏo] *n.* 水牛;水陸坦克

The teacher taught her students to recognize different kinds of buffalo.

這位老師教她的學生辨別數種水牛。

10 swamp [swɑmp] *n.* 沼澤,沼澤地

Shrek is an ogre living in the swamp.

史瑞克是住在沼澤裡的妖怪。

【同】marsh, moor, slough

11 wet [wɛt] *adj.* 濕的

The morning of the examination was wet.

考試的那天上午天氣多雨。

12 ample [ˋæmp!] *adj.* 足夠的;寬敞的

I have ample time to finish my work.

我有足夠的時間完成我的工作。

13 survive [səˋvaɪv] *vt.* 倖免於 *vi.* 活下來

You need to be tough to survive in the jungle.

要在叢林中活下來就要有堅忍不拔的意志。

【同】outlive, outlast, endure, last

14 snake [snek] *n.* 蛇

That girl extremely hates snake.

那個女孩很討厭蛇。

Some snakes are harmless.

一些蛇是無害的。

15 bird [bɝd] *n.* 鳥，禽

The bird is a robin.

這是一隻知更鳥。

16 song [sɔŋ] *n.* 歌曲

We raised our voices in song.

我們放聲歌唱。

folk song 民歌

pop song 流行歌曲

17 wade [wed] *vt.* 趟（河），跋涉

The expedition went across the river.

探險隊涉水過河。

【同】ford

18 prairie [`prɛrɪ] *n.* 大草原，牧場

A single spark can start a prairie fire.

【諺】星星之火可以燎原。

19 roll　[rol]　*vi.*　打滾；滾動

Years rolled on.

歲月流逝。

the rolling stone 正在滾動的石頭

roll over（使）翻滾，打滾

20 sky　[skaɪ]　*n.*　天空

You can see stars in clusters in the night sky.

你可以看到夜空中的星群。

21 hawk　[hɔk]　*n.*　鷹，隼

The hawk is hunting its prey.

鷹正在獵捕牠的獵物。

22 soar　[sor]　*vi.*　高揚，翱翔

The birds soar in the sky.

鳥兒在天上翱翔。

【同】fly, wing, glide

23 burrow　[`bɝo]　*n.*　（兔子等）所掘的地洞　*v.*　挖洞

The rabbit burrowed under the fence.

兔子在籬笆下挖洞。

24 underground　[`ʌndɚ͵graʊnd]　*adj.*　地下的

The cavers discovered a vast underground chamber.

探穴人發現了一個地下大洞穴。

【同】secret, undercover

25 tunnel　[ˋtʌn!]　*n.*　隧道，坑道，地道

The kid dug a tunnel in the sand.

小孩們在沙堆裡挖了一個地道。

【同】passage, passageway

26 den　[dɛn]　*n.*　窩，獸穴

We discovered the bear's den.

我們發現了這隻熊的巢穴。

27 extinct　[ɪkˋstɪŋkt]　*adj.*　絕種的；熄滅了的

Dinosaurs have been extinct for millions of years.

恐龍已絕種幾百萬年了。

【同】gone, dead

28 existence　[ɪgˋzɪstəns]　*n.*　存在，實在；生存

Many people believe in the existence of God.

許多人相信神的存在。

29 creature　[ˋkritʃɚ]　*n.*　生物，動物，家畜

Rain forests are filled with a variety of creatures.

雨林裏頭有很多不同種類的生物。

30 environment　[ɪnˋvaɪrənmənt]　*n.*　環境，外界；圍繞

She gets used to the new environment.

她漸漸習慣新環境。

【同】surrounding, circumstance

Unit
12

Zoo 動物園

1 **entrance** [`ɛntrəns] *n.* 入口；進入；入場

Let's meet at the entrance to the theater.

我們在戲院的門口見。

the entrance to Bear Country 去熊園的入口

win an entrance prize to college 贏得了大學入學獎

2 **ticket** [`tɪkɪt] *n.* 門票；(交通違章) 罰款傳票

The driver was ticketed for parking in front of a fire hydrant.

那個司機因把車停在消防栓前而接到交通違規罰單。

3 **animal** [`ænəm!] *n.* 動物，獸 *adj.* 動物的

Human beings are social animals.

人是社會性的動物。

wild animals 野獸

domestic animals 家畜

4 **cage** [kedʒ] *n.* 畜養禽、獸的籠子

The tiger is locked in the cage.

老虎被關在籠子裡。

escape from the cage 從籠子裡逃跑了

bird cage 鳥籠

5 enclose　[ɪnˋkloz]　*vt.*　圍住，圈起；附上

Please notice that a check is enclosed herewith.

請注意隨信附有支票。

6 scent　[sɛnt]　*n.*　氣味，香味；香水

If we're upwind of the animal it may smell our scent.

要是我們處於那動物的上風位置，它就能聞到我們的氣味。

【同】perfume, fragrance, aroma

主題 2

7 roam　[rom]　*vt.*　在…漫步，漫遊

My boyfriend and I roam around the city.

我和我男朋友在城市漫遊。

8 elephant　[ˋɛləfənt]　*n.*　象

My brother likes to visit elephants in the zoo.

我弟弟喜歡看動物園裡的大象。

white elephant 無用而又難於處理的東西

African elephant 非洲的大象

9 wolf　[wʊlf]　*n.*　狼

She is interested in wolves and werewolves.

她對狼和狼人有興趣。

10 fodder　[ˋfɑdɚ]　*n.*　草料

Food and fodder should go ahead of troops and horses.

【諺】兵馬不動，糧草先行。

11 **bran**　[bræn]　*n.*　糠，麩

This breakfast cereal has added bran.
這個早餐麥片添加了麩皮。

12 **grass**　[græs]　*n.*　草；草地

They are sitting on the grass.
他們坐在草地上。

feed on grass 以草為食
keep off the grass 請勿踐踏草地

13 **tuft**　[tʌft]　*n.*　一簇，叢生植物

There are only a few tufts of grass on the wasteland.
荒原上只有幾簇草。

14 **chiefly**　[`tʃiflɪ]　*adv.*　主要地

Her concerns are chiefly about money.
她掛念的主要都是錢。

15 **ape**　[ep]　*n.*　猿

Human beings evolved from the apes.
人類是從類人猿演化而來的。
【同】monkey

16 **swing**　[swɪŋ]　*vi.*　搖擺；回轉　*n.*　搖擺

The tree swung in the wind.
樹在風中搖曳。

17 vine [vaɪn] *n.* 葡萄樹；藤

The grapes withered on the vine.
葡萄藤上的葡萄都乾癟了。

18 troop [trup] *vi.* 群集，集合

They trooped into the rally.
他們成群結隊前去參加集會。

19 powerful [`paʊəfəl] *adj.* 強有力的；有權威的

She is a powerful manager in this corporation.
她在這家公司是有權威的經理。

20 breed [brid] *n.* （動物）品種

His horse is of the best breed.
他的馬是最好的品種。

21 herd [hɝd] *n.* 放牧 *vt.* 放牧

Those children just saw a herd of sheep and felt excited.
那些孩子們只是看到一群羊就感到興奮。
Mr. Black trained dogs to herd sheep.
Black 先生訓練狗去牧羊。

22 flock [flɑk] *n.* 羊群，群；大量

Birds of a feather flock together.
【諺】物以類聚。

23 tame　[tem]　*adj.*　馴服的

The dog became tame after a few weeks' training.

狗經過幾週的訓練後，變得溫馴。

24 wild　[waɪld]　*adj.*　野生的；野蠻的

They are wild with excitement.

他們欣喜若狂。

There are wild animals in the forest.

那森林裡有很多野獸。

25 obstinate　[`ɑbstənɪt]　*adj.*　固執的；頑強的

Don't be so obstinate!

別這麼固執！

26 camel　[`kæm!]　*n.*　駱駝

The camel is an herbivorous animal.

駱駝是一種草食動物。

27 ostrich　[`ɑstrɪtʃ]　*n.*　鴕鳥；不接受現實的人

Face the music. Don't be an ostrich.

面對現實吧，不要當鴕鳥心態的人。

28 feather　[`fɛðɚ]　*n.*　羽毛；翎毛；羽狀物

The little boy stuck the feather on his hat.

小男孩把羽毛黏在他的帽子上。

as light as a feather 輕如鴻毛

29 **plume**　[plum]　*n.*　羽毛　*v.*　整理羽毛；搔首弄姿

She holds a fan made of plumes.

她手拿一把由羽毛做成的扇子。

30 **hatch**　[hætʃ]　*vt.*　孵出　*vi.*　（蛋）孵化

Hens' eggs take 21 days to hatch out.

雞蛋需要 21 天才孵化。

【同】breed, incubate

主題 2

主題 3
Education & Fashion
教育與流行

Parenting 教養

Track 25

1 **marriage** [`mærɪdʒ] *n.* 結婚

She met a new guy after the break-up of her marriage.

她婚姻破裂後，認識了新的男人。

Their marriage was a happy one.

他們的婚姻是美滿幸福的。

by marriage 透過婚姻的

marriage of convenience 權宜婚姻（例如為居留權而結婚等）

2 **providence** [`prɑvədəns] *n.* 天意；天命

Maria believed that her husband was sent by providence.

瑪利亞相信她的丈夫是上天送給她的。

divine providence 天意

tempt providence / fate 冒極大的危險

3 **infancy** [`ɪnfənsɪ] *n.* 幼年，初期，幼兒期

Their daughter died in infancy, and they were heartbroken.

他們的女兒在幼年死亡，他們傷心至極。

in its infancy 在初步階段

from infancy 從小

4 beloved [bɪˋlʌvɪd] *adj.* 為…的愛的 *n.* 愛人

I got these flowers from my beloved.

這些花是我心愛的先生送的。

beloved of / by 受到…喜愛

5 tenderness [ˋtɛndɚnɪs] *n.* 柔軟，親切，易觸痛，敏感

Joe's tenderness is really impressive; he always treats girls nicely.

喬的溫柔真是令人印象深刻；他總是很和善地對待女孩。

I love the tenderness of that steak. It's perfect!

我愛極了這塊牛排的柔軟度，太完美了！

6 mercy [ˋmɝsɪ] *n.* 憐憫；寬恕；仁慈

He begged for mercy from the king.

他祈求國王寬恕。

主題 3

7 connection [kəˋnɛkʃən] *n.* 連接，聯繫；連貫性

What is the connection between the two ideas?

這兩個概念之間有何聯繫？

8 dote [dot] *v.* 溺愛，昏聵

George and Kelly dote on their two children and buy them almost everything they ask for.

喬治和凱莉溺愛他們兩個孩子，而且幾乎兩個孩子要什麼就買什麼。

dote on 溺愛

9 **peaceful** [`pisfəl] *adj.* 和平的；安靜的

He is a peaceful man.

他是個性格溫和的人。

peaceful demonstration 和平抗議

10 **kid** [kɪd] *n.* 小孩，兒童，少年

The kid dug a tunnel in the sand.

小孩們在沙堆裡挖了一個地道。

Those kids are so cute that everybody likes them.

那群孩子如此可愛，每個人都喜歡他們。

11 **parent** [`pɛrənt] *n.* 父（母）親

Being a parent can be hard work.

當父母可是件辛苦的事。

see one's parents 見某人的父母親

12 **obligation** [ˌɑbləˋgeʃən] *n.* 義務，職責，責任

I have an obligation not to do this work.

我有義務不做這項工作。

13 **welfare** [`wɛlˌfɛr] *n.* 幸福，福利

This organization is concerned about children's welfare.

這個組織關心孩子的福利。

【同】 wellbeing, health

14 **reasonable** [`riznəb!] *adj.* 有道理的

I think that's not reasonable.

我認為這是沒有道理的。

15 affection　　[əˋfɛkʃən]　　*n.*　　慈愛，愛；愛慕

Peter didn't show his children any affection.

彼得對他的小孩毫不關心。

affection for sb. / sth. 對某人／某物趕到關心或喜愛

16 human　　[ˋhjumən]　　*n.*　　人　　*adj.*　　人的，人類的

The accident was caused by human error.

這宗事故是人為過失造成的。

17 demeanor　　[dɪˋminɚ]　　*n.*　　行為，舉止

His lawyer had a professional demeanor in court.

他的律師在法庭上具有專業的舉止。

18 merry　　[ˋmɛrɪ]　　*adj.*　　歡樂的，愉快的

A merry heart goes all the way.

【諺】心情愉快，萬事順利。

19 curiosity　　[ˌkjʊrɪˋɑsətɪ]　　*n.*　　好奇，好奇心；珍品

The child showed a healthy curiosity.

那孩子有好奇心，這是好現象。

20 affectionate　　[əˋfɛkʃənɪt]　　*adj.*　　摯愛的

Dolly's mother is very affectionate with her.

桃莉的媽媽對她很關愛。

affectionate with / towards / to... 對⋯關愛

an affectionate kiss 深情的吻

21 **mischievous** [ˋmɪstʃɪvəs] *adj.* 淘氣的，有害處的

His mischievous sense of humor is really hurting my feelings.

他傷人的幽默感真的傷了我的心。

22 **demon** [ˋdimən] *n.* 魔鬼

Tom's mother likes to call him a little demon because he never listens to her words.

湯姆的媽媽喜歡叫他小惡魔因為他從不聽她的話。

do sth. like a demon 做某事很厲害

23 **attitude** [ˋætətjud] *n.* 態度，看法；姿勢

A positive attitude is needed if you really want this job.

如果你想要這份工作，就需要積極的態度。

24 **punishment** [ˋpʌnɪʃmənt] *n.* 罰，懲罰，處罰

Although he did something wrong, the punishment was still too harsh.

雖然他做錯了事，這種處罰還是太嚴厲了。

25 **discipline** [ˋdɪsəplɪn] *n.* 紀律；訓練 *vt.* 訓練

The teacher can't keep discipline in her class.

那位老師無法維持教室紀律。

26 manner　[ˋmænɚ]　*n.*　方式；態度；禮貌

It is bad manners to interrupt.

打斷別人說話是不禮貌的。

He has a good manner.

他有一個好習慣。

27 refuse　[rɪˋfjuz]　*vt.*　拒絕　*vt.*　拒絕

I deem it proper to refuse.

我看還是拒絕為好。

refuse to do sth. 拒絕做某事

refuse help 拒絕 明

28 permission　[pɚˋmɪʃən]　*n.*　允許，許可，同意

It is not easy to get my father's permission when I want to go out at night.

我晚上要出門的話，要得到我父親的允許不太容易。

主題 3

29 discretion　[dɪˋskrɛʃən]　*n.*　謹慎，審慎

Use your discretion when you are choosing from these two options.

當你從這兩個選項中選擇時，要謹慎行事。

at sb.'s discretion 由某人決定

30 humility　[hjuˋmɪlətɪ]　*n.*　謙遜，謙恭

I am fond of his humility.

我很喜歡他的謙遜。

Unit
02

Language 語言

 Track 26

1 recite [rɪˋsaɪt] *vi.* *vt.* 背誦；敘述

Can you recite the Ten Commandants?

你能背誦十誡嗎？

2 skim [skɪm] *vt.* 掠過，擦過；略讀

Please skim the article and answer the following question.

請略讀此文章並回答下列問題。

skim through / over 略讀；瀏覽

【同】scan

3 condense [kənˋdɛns] *vt.* 壓縮，使縮短

My teacher helped me condense my report.

我的老師幫我濃縮我的報告。

condense into one page 縮短成一頁

【同】compress, shorten

【反】expand, amplify, extend

4 text [tɛkst] *n.* 課文；課本

He is reading a text on Chinese philosophy.

他在讀一本中國哲學的教科書。

I haven't used my cell phone for three days. When I turned

it on, more than fifty text messages came in.

我有三天沒用手機了。當我一開機，有超過五十則簡訊進來。

5　**topic**　[`tɑpɪk]　*n.*　（文章的）題目；主題

There are many topics that you can choose when you prepare a speech.

當你準備演講時，有很多主題可以選擇。

get back on topic 回到主題

keep it on topic 維持在主題上

【同】subject, theme, issue

6　**sentence**　[`sɛntəns]　*vt.*　判決，宣判　*n.*　句子；判決

This is not a difficult sentence, so why can't you understand it?

這不是個很困難的句子，所以你為什麼就不懂呢？

serve a sentence 服刑

be sentenced to death 遭判死刑

主題 3

7　**phrase**　[frez]　*n.*　短語；習慣用語

This book contains many useful phrases you need when you travel to France.

這本書包含了許多你在法國旅遊時，會需要的有用短語。

coin a phrase 創造一個短句

8　**clause**　[klɔz]　*n.*　子句，條款

This is a coordinate clause.

這是一個並列子句。

9　syllable　[ˋsɪləb!]　*n.*　音節

Which syllable does the stress of this word fall on?

這個字的重音是在哪個音節上？

10　emphasis　[ˋɛmfəsɪs]　*n.*　強調，重點，重要性

Recently, there has been a lot of emphasis on environmental protection.

近來愈來愈強調環保的重要性。

11　gradual　[ˋgrædʒʊəl]　*adj.*　逐漸的；漸進的

Mary finally realized that there had been a gradual change in their relationship.

瑪莉終於了解他們的感情漸漸地變質了。

12　reading　[ˋridɪŋ]　*n.*　讀，閱讀；讀書

My brother is fond of reading, and he can finish a book in a week.

我哥哥很喜歡閱讀，他可以一星期看完一本書。

13　literary　[ˋlɪtəˏrɛrɪ]　*adj.*　精通文學的

I love this writer, who won several literary prizes.

我喜歡這位作家，他贏得不少的文學獎。

literary criticism 文學批評

14　library　[ˋlaɪˏbrɛrɪ]　*n.*　圖書館（室）

It is not a good thing to talk loudly in the library.

在圖書館內大聲說話不是件好事。

15 literature [ˋlɪtərətʃɚ] *n.* 文學；文獻

The lecturer is lecturing on Russian literature.

講師正在講俄羅斯文學。

16 poetry [ˋpoɪtrɪ] *n.* 詩，詩歌，詩作

Poetry is not only his favorite form of literature; he also loves to write it.

詩不只是他最喜歡的文學作品形式，他也非常喜歡寫詩。

17 prose [proz] *n.* 散文

He is a student of prose drama.

他研究散文劇。

18 philosophy [fəˋlɑsəfɪ] *n.* 哲學；哲理；人生觀

He has his own philosophy, so let's not interfere with what he does.

他有他自己的哲理，所以我們不要去干涉他要做什麼。

philosophy of life 人生哲學

19 orator [ˋɔrətɚ] *n.* 演說者，演講者，請願人，原告

He is known as a gifted orator.

眾所周知，他是一位天才演說家。

20 interpreter [ɪnˋtɝprɪtɚ] *n.* 譯員，口譯者

I will be your interpreter this month.

這個月，我將作你的口譯員。

主題 3

21 advanced [əd`vænst] *adj.* 先進的;高級的

This demonstration shows advanced technology to the whole world.
這場展示向全世界呈現了先進的科技。

22 writer [`raɪtə] *n.* 作者,作家,文學家

Do you know who the foremost writer in the English language is?
你知道誰是最重要的英語作家嗎?

23 eloquence [`ɛləkwəns] *n.* 雄辯;口才,修辭

His eloquence impressed all of us, and we all believed in him.
他的口才讓我們所有人都印象深刻,而我們全都信了他的話。
【同】persuasion

24 Latin [`lætɪn] *adj.* 拉丁的 *n.* 拉丁語

Thousands of English words derive from Latin.
英語中有成千上萬的詞源自拉丁文。

25 instruction [ɪn`strʌkʃən] *n.* 命令;教學;教訓

I received great instruction at the local community college I went to.
我在當地社區大學得到很大的指導。
the instructions about keeping food 關於保存食物的說明
do sth. following the instructions 按說明做某事

26 attention [ə`tɛnʃən] *n.* 注意,留心;注意力

You should focus your attention on your work.

你應該把注意力放到工作上。

pay attention to 注意

pay no attention 沒注意

27 effort [ˈɛfɚt] *n.* 努力；努力的成果

The decoration of this house is all her effort. You didn't do anything at all!

這棟房子的裝潢是她努力的結果，你根本沒做什麼事！

make an effort to do sth. 努力做某事

make a great effort to do sth 非常努力做某事

28 practice [ˈpræktɪs] *n.* 實踐；練習；業務

Learning a language takes a lot of practice.

學習語言需要勤練不倦。

be out of practice 缺少練習

put into practice 被付諸實施

29 dialect [ˈdaɪəlɛkt] *n.* 方言，土語，地方話

English is a West Germanic dialect.

英語源自西日爾曼語。

30 intercourse [ˈɪntɚˌkors] *n.* 交際，往來，交流

Most people usually use English in international intercourse, and that's why English is a powerful language.

多數人在國際交流時通常使用英語，這就是為什麼英語是個強勢的語言。

主題 3

Mathematics 數學

Track 27

1 mathematics [ˌmæθəˋmætɪks] *n.* 數學

He is superior to his brother in mathematics.
他的數學比他兄弟好。

2 number [ˋnʌmbə] *vt.* 共計，達…之數

The number of your fingers is ten.
你雙手手指的總數是 10。
the number of people 人的數位
a large number of people 許多人

3 division [dəˋvɪʒən] *n.* 分，分配；除法

Can you do long division?
你會長除法嗎？

4 addition [əˋdɪʃən] *n.* 加，加法；附加物

Addition and division are forms of computation.
加法和除法都是計算方法。

5 series [ˋsiriz] *n.* 連續，系列；叢書

The farmer channel water through a series of irrigation canals.

農夫把水引入一連串的灌溉渠中。

【同】set, cycle, succession

6 rule [rul] *n.* 規則；規定

Do not break the rule.

不要違反規則。

rule over 管理，統治

the spelling rule 拼寫規則

7 relation [rɪˋleʃən] *n.* 關係，聯繫；家屬

I don't see any relation between the two problems.

我看不出這兩個問題間的聯繫。

Their relations appeared to be quite fat.

他們的親戚看起來相當胖。

There is no relationship between the two things.

那兩件事間像是沒有什麼關係。

主題 3

8 reduce [rɪˋdjus] *vt.* 縮減；減少

The windows were tinted to reduce the glare.

窗戶上塗上了淺色以減少強光。

reduce movement to far below the ordinary level 減少運動到遠遠在正常水準之下

9 fraction [ˋfrækʃən] *n.* 小部分；片段；分數

He has done only a fraction of his homework.

他只做了家庭作業的一小部分。

【同】part, bit

10 volume   [`vɑljəm]   *n.*   卷，冊；容積；音量

Is that volume still in print?

那本書還能買到嗎？

11 distance   [`dɪstəns]   *n.*   距離；遠處

They saw a few houses in the distance.

他們看到遠處有幾所房子。

in the distance 在遠處

12 symbol   [`sɪmb!]   *n.*   象徵；符號，記號

The dove is the symbol of peace.

鴿子是和平的象徵。

【同】emblem, token, sign

13 study   [`stʌdɪ]   *v.*   學習

I like to study in the library.

我喜歡在圖書館學習。

an hour's study 一個小時的學習

in one's study 在書房裡

14 marvelous   [`mɑrvələs]   *adj.*   令人驚異的，了不起的，不平常的

He had the most marvelous experience when he was in Africa.

當他在非洲時，他有過極奇特的經歷。

15 **wonder** [ˋwʌndɚ] *n.* 驚異，驚奇；奇跡

They kept looking at the strange sight in silent wonder.

他們驚訝地默默一直盯著那奇景。

in wonder 在驚訝中

wonder about sb. 想瞭解某人

wonder if... 想知道是否…

16 **school** [skul] *n.* 學校

Which school does your child go to?

你的孩子在哪所學校念書？

17 **college** [ˋkɑlɪdʒ] *n.* （綜合大學中的）學院

She studies at a medical college in New York.

她在紐約的一所醫學院學習。

go to college 上大學

leave college 離開大學，大學畢業

主題 3

18 **genius** [ˋdʒinjəs] *n.* 天才；天才人物

He is a mathematical genius.

他是一個數學天才。

【同】talent, gift, capacity

【反】idiot

19 **infinite** [ˋɪnfənɪt] *n.* 無限；無窮（大）

I can see that her future is infinite.

我可以看見她的未來是無限的。

【同】boundless, vast, unlimited

20 innumerable [ɪˋnjumərəb!] *adj.* 無數的，數不清的

Carrie is a great swimmer, and she has won innumerable prizes.

凱莉是個很厲害的游泳選手，她贏過無數的獎項。

21 naught [nɔt] *n.* 無，零，無用

I believe that all our efforts will not go for naught.

我相信我們的努力不會毫無結果。

22 uncertain [ʌnˋsɝtn] *adj.* 無常的；不確定的

The time of his arrival is uncertain.

他抵達的時間尚未確定。

【同】capricious, erratic, fickle

23 probable [ˋprɑbəb!] *adj.* 或有的；大概的

It is very probable that they will win the competition.

他們很可能會贏得這場競爭賽。

24 rough [rʌf] *adj.* 表面不平的；粗略的

I had a rough idea where the missing child was.

我大約知道失蹤的孩子在哪裡。

take the rough with the smooth 風雨與共

25 population [ˌpɑpjəˋleʃən] *n.* 人口；全體居民

The world has a growing population, so we need more food.

這個世界的人口在增長，因此我們需要更多食物。

population explosion 人口爆炸

dense / sparse population 人口眾多／稀少

26 plenty [ˋplɛntɪ] *n.* 充足；大量

I answered this question with plenty of quotations.

我用了大量引文回答這個問題。

in plenty 數量充足

27 surpass [səˋpæs] *vt.* 超過，超越，勝過

Zoe surpassed her brother in physics.

柔伊在物理方面超過了她的兄弟。

surpass oneself 超越自己

主題 3

28 perplex [pəˋplɛks] *vt.* 迷惑，困惑，難住

When a new course was introduced, many parents were perplexed by it.

當引進新課程時，許多家長對此感到迷惑不解。

29 proposition [͵prɑpəˋzɪʃən] *n.* 命題，主題；提議

The proposition was voted on and became company policy.

這項提議付諸表決並成為公司的政策。

30 admit [ədˋmɪt] *vt.* *vi.* 承認

I must admit that he is a competent man.

我必須承認他是個能幹的人。

Art 藝術

 Track 28

1 artistic [ɑr`tɪstɪk] *adj.* 藝術的；藝術家的

She always deals with everything in an artistic manner.
她總是以一種藝術家的態度來處理所有事。

My father collects many artistic works.
我爸爸蒐集很多藝術品。

2 unknown [ʌn`non] *adj.* 不為人所知的

The cause of the delay is as yet unknown.
延遲的原因目前還不知道。

3 leisure [`liʒɚ] *n.* 閒置時間；悠閒

What do you often do in your leisure time?
你閒暇時常做什麼？

【同】relaxation, rest, retirement

4 illustration [ɪ,lʌs`treʃən] *n.* 說明，圖解；例證

The illustrations of this book are very delicate.
這本書的插圖很精緻。

by way of illusion 用例子

5 object [`ɑbdʒɪkt] *n.* 物，物體；目的

Various objects were on the table.

桌子上擺著各種各樣的物體。

a direct object 直接賓語

an indirect object 間接賓語

6 likeness [`laɪknɪs] *n.* 同樣；類似，相似

Do you find any family likeness between these two brothers?

這兩兄弟之間，你有發現任何家族的相似點嗎？

7 respectful [rɪ`spɛktfəl] *adj.* 恭敬的，尊重的

He is always respectful of my opinions.

他總是尊重我的意見。

主題 **3**

8 glorify [`glorə,faɪ] *vt.* 讚美（上帝）；頌揚

Many people think that this film glories violence.

很多人認為這部電影頌揚暴力。

9 extol [ɪk`stol] *v.* 讚美

My father keeps extolling Becky's sweetness.

我爸爸對蓓琪的甜美讚不絕口。

【同】exalt, laud, praise

10 expression [ɪk`sprɛʃən] *n.* 詞句；表達；表情

Tommy had an indifferent expression on his face.

湯米的臉上有一種事不關己的表情。

11 **illustrate** [ˋɪləstret] *vt.* （用圖等）說明

Justin used the diagram to illustrate his point.

賈斯汀使用圖表來說明他的論點。

【同】exemplify, explain, elucidate

12 **sketch** [skɛtʃ] *n.* 略圖；速寫；概略

His sketch of the scenery is really good.

他的風景速寫非常的棒。

【同】drawing, vignette, design

13 **diffuse** [dɪˋfjuz] *vt. vi.* 使（熱）散開

The light was diffused by the leaves.

樹葉使光線漫射。

14 **shadow** [ˋʃædo] *n.* 影子

The barking dog cast its shadow on the wall.

那隻在叫的狗影子映在牆上。

in the shadows 在陰影下

under the shadow of sth. 在…的陰影／影響之下

in sb.'s shadow 在某人的陰影下／不如某人

15 **coarse** [kors] *adj.* 粗的，粗糙的

The orphan's dress was made of coarse cloth.

那名孤兒的洋裝是用粗布製成的。

16 fine [faɪn] *adj.* 好的 *adv.* 很好，妙

She is really a fine artist.

她真是一位傑出的藝術家。

fine clothes 漂亮的衣服

fine rain 細雨

17 impression [ɪm`prɛʃən] *n.* 印；印象；印記

Her kindness has given me a deep impression.

她的善良給我留下了很深的印象。

【同】feeling, memory

18 illusion [ɪ`ljuʒən] *n.* 幻想；錯覺；假像

A mirage is an optical illusion.

海市蜃樓是一種視錯覺。

【同】delusion, fantasy, error

19 fertile [`fɝtl] *adj.* 肥沃的；多產的

France is a very fertile area for grapes.

法國是一個多產葡萄的地區。

20 original [ə`rɪdʒənl] *adj.* 最初的；新穎的

The original picture is in the British Museum.

這幅畫的原作在大英博物館內。

21 marvel [`mɑrvl] *n.* 奇跡；驚奇 *vt.* 驚奇

They marveled that Sally would make such a choice.

他們對於莎莉會做出這樣的選擇而感到驚訝。

22 exquisite　[`ɛkskwɪzɪt]　*adj.*　精緻的，近完美的

Her wedding dress has very exquisite lace.

她的結婚禮服有非常精緻的花邊。

exquisite taste 高尚的品味

exquisite craftsmanship 精湛的工藝

【同】delicate, elaborate

【反】coarse, crude

23 canvas　[`kænvəs]　*n.*　粗帆布；一塊油畫布

There are blobs of paint dotted around the canvas.

油畫布上佈滿了顏料。

24 masterpiece　[`mæstəˌpis]　*n.*　傑作，名著

It is one of the great masterpieces of European art.

它是歐洲藝術最傑出的作品之一。

25 perfect　[`pɝfɪkt]　*adj.*　極好的，完美的

Luna was a perfect girl in her boyfriend's eyes.

在她男友眼裡，露娜是一個完美的女孩。

perfect timing 時間抓得剛剛好

perfect for 對…是非常合適的

26 true　[tru]　*adj.*　真的；忠實的

She was always true to her word.

她總是信守諾言的。

be true 是真的

be true to sb. 忠實於某人

27 critic [`krɪtɪk] *n.* 批評家，愛挑剔的人

A critic is a man whose watch is five minutes ahead of other people's.

【諺】批評家是手錶比別人快上五分鐘的人。

music / literary / film critic 樂評／文評／影評人

armchair critic 只會批評不會做事的人

28 authority [ə`θɔrətɪ] *n.* 當局，官方；權力

The government is the highest authority in the country.

政府是國家的最高權力機構。

29 consecrate [`kɑnsɪ,kret] *vt.* 供神用，奉獻，使神聖

George consecrated his life to art.

喬治獻身於藝術。

Her aunt consecrated her life to God.

她的阿姨將自己的生命獻給上帝。

【同】dedicate, devote

30 immortality [,ɪmɔr`tælətɪ] *n.* 不朽，不朽的聲名

The professor has achieved immortality.

那位教授獲得了永垂不朽的聲名。

Michael Jackson enjoyed immortality in show business.

麥克傑克森在演藝界享有永恆不朽的地位。

主題 3

Music 音樂

 Track 29

1 universal [͵junə`vɝs!] *adj.* 宇宙的；普遍的

Football is a universal game.

足球是一項全球性的運動。

2 musical [`mjuzɪk!] *adj.* 音樂的

He can play nearly every musical instrument.

他幾乎能夠演奏每一種樂器。

Sally is very musical and loves to sing.

莎莉很有音樂細胞而且愛唱歌。

3 festival [`fɛstəv!] *n.* 節日；音樂節

Sherry managed the planning of the festival.

雪莉管理節日活動的籌畫。

4 record [`rɛkəd] *n.* 記錄，記載；唱片

My husband keeps a record of our everyday expenses.

我丈夫將日常開銷都記錄下來。

keep a record 記錄下來

put sth. on record 記錄某事

break a record 打破紀錄

5　instrument　[`ɪnstrəmənt]　*n.*　儀器；工具；樂器

The compass is an instrument of navigation.

羅盤是航行儀器。

6　bugle　[`bjug!]　*n.*　軍號，喇叭

Morris blew two or three notes on his bugle.

莫里斯吹了兩三聲喇叭。

blow a bugle 吹奏喇叭

7　flute　[flut]　*n.*　笛子

That young man took out his flute and played it.

那位年輕人拿出笛子吹了起來。

He played a flute and it was really beautiful.

他吹奏笛子，真的很好聽。

主題 3

8　fife　[faɪf]　*n.*　橫笛，吹橫笛

That little boy is good at playing the fife.

那名小男孩善於吹橫笛。

George is learning to play the fife.

喬治正在學習如何吹奏橫笛。

9　lute　[lut]　*n.*　琵琶，封泥

My sister knows how to play the Chinese lute.

我妹妹會彈中國琵琶。

In ancient China, there was a beautiful woman who was famous for playing the lute.

在古代中國，有一位美女以彈奏琵琶聞名。

10 **piano** [pɪˋæno] *n.* 鋼琴

He is a wizard at playing the piano.
他是個鋼琴奇才。

11 **violin** [ˌvaɪəˋlɪn] *n.* 小提琴

That violin has a beautiful tone.
那支小提琴的音色很美。

12 **popular** [ˋpɑpjələ] *adj.* 大眾的；流行的

Many young people love to sing popular songs at KTV.
許多年輕人喜愛在 KTV 唱流行歌曲。
be popular with (among) sb. 很受某人的歡迎

13 **pop** [pɑp] *n.* 流行音樂，流行歌曲

I have no interest in pop music.
我對流行音樂不感興趣。

14 **musician** [mjuˋzɪʃən] *n.* 音樂家；作曲家

Robert is a very talented musician.
羅伯特是很有天份的音樂家。

15 **western** [ˋwɛstɚn] *adj.* 西的，西方的

I like movies, but I don't like Westerns.
我喜歡電影，但不喜歡西部牛仔片。

16 opera [`ɑpərə] *n.* 歌劇

Have you heard the opera sung in Italian?

你聽過用義大利語唱的這場歌劇嗎？

17 classical [`klæsɪk!] *adj.* 古典的；經典的

Beethoven is seen as one of the masters of classical music.

貝多芬被認為是古典音樂大師之一。

My sister showed an interest in classical literature when she was ten years old.

我妹妹十歲的時候展現出對古典文學有興趣。

18 conductor [kən`dʌktɚ] *n.* 售票員；（樂隊）指揮

The young soprano was encouraged by a famous conductor.

那年輕的女高音歌手受到一著名指揮家的鼓勵。

The conductor is very important in a musical concert.

在音樂會中，指揮是很重要的。

19 orchestra [`ɔrkɪstrə] *n.* 管弦樂隊

The orchestra has several concert engagements on the way.

這管弦樂隊有許多音樂會準備表演。

Her sister plays the flute in the school orchestra.

她妹妹在學校的管弦樂隊中吹奏笛子。

主題 3

20 choir [kwaɪr] *n.* （教堂的）歌唱隊

The choir is the most famous part of that church.
唱詩班是那個教堂最著名的部分。

21 vocal [ˋvok!] *adj.* 聲音的，有聲的，歌唱的

We have to take care of our vocal chords.
我們必須好好照顧我們的聲帶。

22 rhyme [raɪm] *n.* 韻，押韻，韻文

Is there a rhyme for rainbow?
有和 rainbow 押韻的詞嗎？
in rhyme 押韻
no rhyme or reason 毫無道理或組織

23 melody [ˋmɛlədɪ] *n.* 旋律，曲調；歌曲

The singer is well-known for her songs with plaintive melodies.
這名歌手以她歌曲中的曲調悲傷而聞名。

24 hum [hʌm] *n.* 嗡嗡聲 *vt.* 哼曲子

Why don't you hum the opening bars of your favorite tune, and I'll see if I know it.
何不哼一哼你喜愛曲子的開頭幾小節，我看看我知不知道。

25 theme [θim] *n.* 題目；詞幹；主旋律

The main theme of the article is not clear.
這篇文章的主題不明。
【同】subject, topic, thread

26 airy [ˋɛrɪ] *adj.* 空氣的，幻想的，輕快的

The airy tune sounds very nice to the ears.

這首輕快的曲子聽起來非常悅耳。

Our new office is light and airy.

我們新的辦公室很明亮寬敞。

27 ballad [ˋbæləd] *n.* 歌謠，小曲

My grandparents enjoy ballads instead of pop music.

我的祖父母喜歡民歌，而非流行音樂。

He likes to sing ballads to his girlfriend.

他喜歡唱歌謠給女朋友聽。

主題 3

28 perfection [pɚˋfɛkʃən] *n.* 盡善盡美；無比精確

She had practiced a lot and played the music to perfection.

她充分練習並把這支樂曲演奏的完美無缺。

29 ecstasy [ˋɛkstəsɪ] *n.* 狂喜，心醉神怡

The audience watched the concert with ecstasy.

觀眾看著演唱會看得入神。

in ecstasy 在狂喜中

go into ecstasies 變得非常開心

30 rapture [ˋræptʃɚ] *n.* 狂喜，歡天喜地

Marco fell into raptures over rock music.

馬可對搖滾樂喜愛若狂。

in rapture 歡天喜地的狀態中

Unit
06

Testing 考試

1 test [tɛst] *n. vt.* 測驗，考查

The teacher will test us in math.

老師將測驗我們數學。

2 quiz [kwɪz] *n.* 小型考試，測驗

We will have a quiz this Friday.

我們這個星期五有一個小考。

3 attest [əˋtɛst] *v.* 證明

The success of that businesswoman attests to her ability.

那位女商人的成功證明了她的能力。

The expensive furniture in their house attested to their wealth.

他們家裡昂貴的家具證明了他們的財力。

【同】certify, testify

4 indifferent [ɪnˋdɪfərənt] *adj.* 冷漠的；不積極的

I don't understand why Jerry is indifferent to the result of the exam.

我不懂為什麼傑瑞對於考試結果漠不關心。

Maria is quite indifferent to Tom, and that hurts his feelings.

瑪莉亞對湯姆相當冷漠，這很傷她的心。

【同】cold, chilly, apathetic

【反】interested

5 **imperfect** [ɪmˋpɝfɪkt] *adj.* 有缺點的，半完成的，減弱的

The world is imperfect, so we always need to put up with something.

這個世界是不完美的，所以我們總必須忍受。

【同】faulty, flawed, broken

6 **attendance** [əˋtɛndəns] *n.* 到場；出席人數

The meeting requires everyone's attendance.

這場會議需要每個人出席。

【同】alertness, concentration

7 **additional** [əˋdɪʃən!] *adj.* 附加的，追加的

We need additional material to complete the job.

我們需要額外的素材來完成這項工作。

additional cost / expenditure 額外支出

8 **sure** [ʃʊr] *adj.* 確信的，肯定的

She is sure to pass the examination.

她一定會通過考試。

be sure of... 確信…

be sure that... 確信…

be sure of oneself 有自信

主題 **3**

9 fail [fel] *vi.* 失敗

Our plan has failed, and everyone is sad.

我們的計畫失敗了，而每個人都很傷心。

fail one's exam 考試不及格

fail to do sth. 做某事沒成功

fail sb. 讓某人失望

10 severe [sə`vɪr] *adj.* 嚴格的；嚴厲的

That boy just broke a vase and should not get such severe punishment.

那男孩只是打破花瓶而已，不應該接受到如此嚴厲的處罰。

11 terrible [`tɛrəb!] *adj.* 可怕的；極度的

The earthquake was so terrible that we were speechless.

這次地震好可怕，我們都無言了。

terrible film 可怕的（壞的）電影

terrible weather 壞天氣

12 terror [`tɛrɚ] *n.* 恐怖，驚駭

The horse bolted in terror when it heard the sound of the gun.

當馬兒聽到槍聲時，牠嚇壞了。

13 negative [`nɛgətɪv] *adj.* 負的，陰性的

When I asked him to my party, he gave me a negative answer.

當我邀他來參加我的派對，他給了我一個否定的答案。

14 error [`ɛrə] *n.* 錯誤，謬誤；差錯

You don't need to be responsible for this error which was made by the printer.

你不需要為這個錯誤負責，這是由印刷工人造成的。

15 disappoint [ˌdɪsəˋpɔɪnt] *vt.* 使失望，使受挫折

Please don't disappoint me.

請別讓我感到失望。

16 ignorant [`ɪgnərənt] *adj.* 不知道的；無知的

I'm ignorant of his involvement in the crime.

我對他涉入的犯罪一無所知。

Jeff is an ignorant person.

傑夫是無知的人。

主題 3

17 correct [kəˋrɛkt] *adj.* 正確的 *vt.* 糾正

Is this answer correct?

這個答案正確嗎？

The teacher corrected my composition.

老師批改了我的作業。

18 studious [`stjudɪəs] *adj.* 愛好學問的，努力的，故意的

My brother is never a studious student.

我弟弟從來不是一個勤奮的學生。

19 apt　[æpt]　*adj.*　恰當的；聰明的

Jeff is a clever boy but apt to get into trouble.

傑夫是個聰明的孩子，卻很容易惹麻煩。

apt to do sth. 容易做某事

apt for 適合

20 smart　[smɑrt]　*adj.*　巧妙的；灑脫的

You look smart in the new suit.

你穿這套新衣服很帥氣。

21 wise　[waɪz]　*adj.*　有智慧的，聰明的

You are wise to remain silent.

你保持沉默，這很明智。

wise advice 賢明的忠告

22 intellectual　[ˌɪnt!ˋɛktʃʊəl]　*n.*　知識份子　*adj.*　智力的

Chess is a highly intellectual game.

象棋是需用高度智力的運動專案。

【同】academic, scholarly

23 advancement　[ədˋvænsmənt]　*n.*　前進，進步

The purpose of a university is the advancement of learning.

大學的目標是使學習更進一步。

24 wisdom　[ˋwɪzdəm]　*n.*　（古人的）名言，格言

He is not a man with worldly wisdom.

他不是一個有處世才能的人。

25 determine [dɪ`tɝmɪn] vt. 決定；查明；決心

The exam results could determine your career.

考試成績可能會決定你的前途。

be determined to become 已決心成為…

be determined to do sth. 決定做某事

26 correction [kə`rɛkʃən] n. 改正，糾正，修改

The teacher made quite a few corrections to my paper.

老師對於我的報告做了不少修正。

27 comprehend [ˌkɑmprɪ`hɛnd] vt. 瞭解，理解，領會

I cannot comprehend this phrase.

我無法理解這個片語。

主題 3

28 emerge [ɪ`mɝdʒ] vi. 出現，湧現；冒出

The moon emerged from behind the clouds.

月亮從雲層後面露出來了。

emerge from 從…出現

emerge as 以…姿態出現

29 glee [gli] n. 歡喜，高興

Those boys shouted with glee when they saw their mother.

那群男孩看到他們的母親時非常高興地叫起來。

30 greatness [`gretnɪs] n. 偉大；巨大

The statue is a reminder of Napoleon's greatness.

這尊雕像使人緬懷拿破崙的偉大功績。

Unit
07

Astrology 占星學

Track 31

1 superstition [ˌsupəˈstɪʃən] *n.* 迷信；盲目崇拜

One of his superstitions is to always put his right shoe on first.

他的迷信之一，是要先穿上他右腳的鞋。

Some people think religion is really just superstition.

有些人認為宗教是真的只是迷信。

superstitionist 醉心於迷信的人

to eliminate superstition 破除迷信

2 antiquity [ænˈtɪkwətɪ] *n.* 古代；古人們

The real meaning is lost in antiquity.

真正的含義已在古代遺失。

antique shop 骨董店

3 celestial [sɪˈlɛstʃəl] *adj.* 天體的，天上的 *n.* 神仙

Venus is a celestial body.

金星是天體中的一員。

celestial globe 星象儀，天球儀

4 prophesy [ˈprɑfəˌsaɪ] *vt.* *vi.* 預言，預報

He prophesied of strange things to come.

他預言將有怪事發生。

prophecy 預言能力

5 **foresee** [for`si] *vt.* 預見，預知，看穿

He foresaw the housing bubble and sold his house.

他預知到了房地產泡沫且把他的房子先賣掉。

foreseer 有先見之明的人

6 **hereafter** [ˌhɪr`æftə] *n.* 將來，來世

He believes that he will live forever in the hereafter.

他相信在來世他會長生不老。

7 **destiny** [`dɛstənɪ] *n.* 命運，天數

It's your destiny to be a teacher.

成為一名教師是你的命運。

destined for 指定

8 **salvation** [sæl`veʃən] *n.* 得救，拯救

Finding the right way to do this was my salvation.

找到正確的方式去做事是我的救星。

9 **peculiar** [pɪ`kjuljə] *adj.* 特有的；特別的 *n.* 特權

We all have our peculiar ways of doing things.

我們都有我們特有的方式做事。

peculiar galaxy 特殊星系

peculiar people 上帝特選的子民

10 **fate** [fet] *n.* 命運，天數

He believes he is fated for greatness.

他認為他是生來註定的偉大。

believe in fate 相信命運

fate line 命運線

11 **intelligence** [ɪnˋtɛlədʒəns] *n.* 智力；理解力；情報

He's the equal of his sister as far as intelligence in concerned.

論智力，他和他姊姊不相上下。

12 **mutter** [ˋmʌtə] *vi.* 輕聲低語；抱怨 *vt.* 抱怨地說 *n.* 咕噥

He muttered about the additional work she gave him.

他抱怨她給的額外工作。

mutter to yourself 自己咕噥著

mutter against 抱怨

13 **deny** [dɪˋnaɪ] *vt.* 否定；拒絕相信

His bid for the presidency was denied.

他擔任主席的申請被拒絕。

deny oneself 節制，戒除

14 **argue** [ˋɑrgjʊ] *vi.* 爭論，爭辯，辯論 *vt.* 議論；主張

They often argue about even the smallest things.

他們常常爭辯即使是芝麻小事。

argue a matter out 把事情查個水落石出

15 **stupid**　[`stjupɪd]　*adj.*　愚蠢的；感覺遲鈍的　*n.*　笨蛋

Why grumble at her about your own stupid mistakes?

你自己犯了愚蠢的錯誤，為什麼向她抱怨？

stupid assumptions 愚蠢的假設

16 **worthless**　[`wɝθlɪs]　*adj.*　無價值的，無用的

That is fools' gold; it is worthless.

這是假的，它不值錢。

17 **ignorance**　[`ɪgnərəns]　*n.*　無知，無學，愚昧

Ignorance of the law is no excuse.

對法律的無知不是藉口。

主題 3

18 **disorder**　[dɪs`ɔrdɚ]　*n.*　混亂，雜亂；騷亂　*vt.*　使紊亂

The course terminated in disorder.

課程在混亂中結束。

disorderly conduct 行為不檢

disorderly house 賭場

19 **childish**　[`tʃaɪldɪʃ]　*adj.*　孩子的；幼稚的

That was a childish thing to say to her.

對她來說這是一個幼稚的事情。

childish pranks in the presence of guests 人來瘋

20 **curse**　[kɝs]　*n.*　咒語　*vt.*　使遭難　*vi.*　詛咒，咒

Their tribe is under a curse.

他們的部落正受詛咒。

curses come home to roost 詛咒他人應驗自己

21 contrary [ˋkɑntrɛrɪ] *n.* 相反；對立面 *adj.* 相反的 *adv.* 反對地

His opinion is always contrary to mine.
他的意見永遠跟我是相反的。

22 motive [ˋmotɪv] *n.* 動機 *adj.* 發動的，運動的 *vt.* 激起

There was no apparent motive for the crime.
沒有明顯的犯罪動機。

Doing well motivated him to practice harder.
表現不俗更激勵他努力練習。

23 unity [ˋjunətɪ] *n.* 單一；統一；團結

There is a lack of unity in our division.
我們部門缺乏的是團結。

24 spiritual [ˋspɪrɪtʃʊəl] *adj.* 精神的，心靈的 *n.* （黑人的）聖歌

He is a spiritual person even though he doesn't go to church.
他是一個信教的人，儘管他沒有去教堂。

25 meditation [͵mɛdəˋteʃən] *n.* 沉思，冥想

He is in deep meditation.
他陷入沉思中。

transcendental meditation 冥思靜坐

meditation hall 禪室

26 **consciousness** [`kɑnʃəsnɪs] *n.* 意識，覺悟；知覺

The patient lost consciousness.

病人失去了知覺。

He lost consciousness briefly after the accident.

他在事故發生後失去了短暫知覺。

27 **prayer** [prɛr] *n.* 祈禱，祈求

He was a great believer in the power of prayer.

他篤信祈禱的力量。

主題 3

28 **holy** [`holɪ] *adj.* 神聖的；聖潔的

Healing is one of the holiest tasks.

醫治是最神聖的工作之一。

29 **solace** [`sɑlɪs] *n.* 安慰，慰藉

He was a great solace to her in her time of need.

在她需要的時候，他是她極大的安慰。

30 **saint** [sent] *n.* 聖徒；基督教徒

Saint Christopher is the patron saint of travellers.

聖徒克里斯多夫是旅行者的守護神。

That man is a saint; he takes so much time to help everybody.

這男子是聖人；他給了這麼多時間來幫助大家。

Unit
08

Style 流行款式

Track 32

1 **apparel** [əˋpærəl] *n.* （精緻的）衣服 *vt.* 給…穿衣服

We sell a full range of men's apparel.

我們有賣一系列的男士服裝。

ladies' apparel 女士服裝

apparent availability 市場表面供應量

2 **attire** [əˋtaɪr] *vt.* 使穿著，裝扮 *n.* 衣服

Waiters' attire is traditionally black and white.

服務員的服裝是傳統的黑色和白色。

attire in 穿上

3 **garment** [ˋgɑrmənt] *n.* 衣服；服裝，衣著 *vt.* 給…穿衣服

Her garments usually come from Paris.

她的服裝通常是從巴黎來。

garment district 服裝區

garment bag 保護衣服用的塑膠套

4 **fashion** [ˋfæʃən] *n.* 樣子，方式；風尚 *vt.* 製作

He's a dedicated follower of fashion.

他是個時尚追隨者。

fashion into 塑造成

5 graceful [`gresfəl] *adj.* 優美的，優雅的

The woman's every movement is very graceful.

那女人的一舉一動都很優雅。

6 comely [`kʌmlɪ] *adj.* 動人的，美麗的

To him, she was the most comely woman; he couldn't take his eyes off her.

對他來說，她是最漂亮的女人；他無法把他的視線從她的身上移開。

7 majestic [mə`dʒɛstɪk] *adj.* 雄偉的；壯麗的

The mountains rose majestically from the plains.

山脈從平原雄偉的上升。

majestic-looking 威風凜凜

8 allure [mə`dʒɛstɪk] *vt.* 引誘 *vi.* 吸引人 *n.* 誘惑力

He can't resist the allure of the big city.

他無法抵抗大城市的吸引力。

allure sb. from 誘使某人離開

9 radiant [`redjənt] *adj.* 絢麗的；容光煥發的 *n.* 發光的物體

She looked absolutely radiant on her wedding day.

在她的婚禮當天，她看起來絕對光芒四射。

radiant energy 輻射能

主題 3

10 divine [dəˋvaɪn] *adj.* 神的；敬神的 *vt.* 占卜；預言 *vi.* （憑直覺）發現

My mother asked me to attend the divine service.

我媽媽要求我做禮拜。

11 bridal [ˋbraɪd!] *adj.* 新娘的，婚禮的 *n.* 婚禮

She had on all her bridal decorations.

她穿戴著所有的新娘裝飾品。

12 lovely [ˋlʌvlɪ] *adj.* 可愛的；好看的

It's a lovely day, not too hot.

是個好天，不太熱。

It was a lovely party.

那是一個令人愉快的晚會。

13 outfit [ˋaʊt,fɪt] *n.* 用具，配備；衣服 *vt.* 裝備 *vi.* 獲得裝備

She wore a different outfit every day.

她每天穿不同的衣服。

14 muse [mjuz] *vt.* 沉思 *vi.* 沉思，默想，冥想

She was the painter's muse.

她是畫家的靈感。

muse about 沉思

15 gentleman [ˋdʒɛnt!mən] *n.* 紳士；有教養的人

He is always a perfect gentleman.

他永遠是完美的紳士。

gentleman in waiting 王室的侍從

gentleman of long robe 律師

16 handsome　[`hænsəm]　_adj._　漂亮的；清秀的；堂皇的

He is a handsome man.

他是個美男子。

17 noble　[`nob!]　_adj._　貴族的；高尚的　_n._　貴族

He is a man of noble birth.

他生為貴族。

noble intentions 崇高的意圖

noble metal 貴金屬

noble-minded 高尚的，高潔的

18 admirable　[`ædmərəb!]　_adj._　可欽佩的，優良的，令人驚奇的

The restaurant is admirable in respect of style.

這家餐廳風格極佳。

admirable courage 令人欽佩的勇氣

19 brotherly　[`brʌðəlɪ]　_adj._　兄弟的，兄弟般的，親切的

He has a very brotherly manner towards the boy.

他像哥哥一樣對待那個男孩。

brotherly affection 手足之愛

brotherly love 兄弟之愛

20 singular [ˋsɪŋɡjələ] *adj.* 非凡的;奇異的 *n.* 【文】單數

That is a singular use of that color.

那是奇異的使用該顏色。

a singular style 奇異的樣式

singular point 奇點

21 quaint [kwent] *adj.* 古雅的;奇特有趣的;奇怪的

What a quaint little building!

多麼古雅的一座小房子啊!

22 temptation [tɛmpˋteʃən] *n.* 誘惑,引誘

I can't resist the temptation.

我不能抵擋誘惑。

give in to temptation 經不住誘惑

23 esteem [ɪsˋtim] *n.* 尊敬,尊重 *vt.* 尊敬;認為

He is my esteemed colleague.

他是我尊敬的同事。

self-esteem 自尊

24 tendency [ˋtɛndənsɪ] *n.* 趨向,趨勢;傾向

The general tendency of the people is to follow their leaders.

人們傾向追隨領導者。

25 vulgar [`vʌlgə] *adj.* 粗俗的，庸俗的 *n.* 平民百姓

It is vulgar to slurp soup directly from the bowl.

咕嚕咕嚕地把碗裡的湯喝完是很粗俗的。

26 excessive [ɪk`sɛsɪv] *adj.* 過多的，極度的

Her use of perfume is always excessive.

她總是使用過量的香水。

excessive consumption 過度消費

excessive expenditure 超支

excessive rainfall 雨水過多

27 ridiculous [rɪ`dɪkjələs] *adj.* 荒謬的，可笑的

Those shoes look ridiculous with that outfit.

那雙鞋在這身衣服上看起來很荒謬。

主題 3

28 false [fɔls] *adj.* 不真實的；偽造的

What she's saying is totally false.

她所說的一切都是假的。

29 fade [fed] *vi.* 褪色；逐漸消失 *vt.* 使褪色

Her suntan is fading.

她曬黑的肌膚開始變淺。

30 insignificant [ˌɪnsɪg`nɪfəkənt] *adj.* 無意義的；低微的

In the long run, what we're doing is insignificant.

長遠來說，我們正在做什麼是微不足道的。

Cosmetics 化妝品

 Track 33

1　model　[ˋmɑd!]　*n.*　模型；模式；模特兒　*vt.*　做⋯的模型
vi.　當模特兒

My brother went whole hog when he became interested in
model airplanes.
我弟弟對模型飛機感興趣之後，就全力以赴了。

2　hasten　[ˋhesn]　*vt.*　催促　*vi.*　趕緊

We must hasten to finish this project.
我們必須盡快完成這個專案。
Smoking will hasten the onset of some diseases.
吸煙會加速一些疾病的發作。
haste makes waste 欲速則不達

3　hastily　[ˋhestɪlɪ]　*adv.*　匆忙地，急速地，慌張地

The pie was hastily made.
派是匆忙做成的。

4　splash　[splæʃ]　*vt.*　*n.*　濺，潑，飛濺

The baby loved to splash in the water.
寶寶愛玩潑水。

5 goodly [ˋgʊdlɪ] *adj.* 漂亮的，可觀的

A goodly portion of that medication is alcohol.

這種藥物佔很大部分是酒精。

【同】considerable；much

6 moist [mɔɪst] *adj.* 濕潤的；多雨的

The clothes are still moist. Dry them in the sun.

這些衣服還是濕的，把它們在太陽下晾乾。

keep moist 保持濕潤

moisture regain 回潮

7 mixture [ˋmɪkstʃɚ] *n.* 混合；混合物

Do you know the constituents of the mixture?

你知道這種混合物的成分嗎？

主題 3

8 eyebrow [ˋaɪˏbraʊ] *n.* 眉毛

He raised an eyebrow at Jack.

他揚起眉毛看著傑克。

pluck your eyebrows 拔你的眉毛

9 underneath [ˏʌndɚˋniθ] *prep.* 在…下面 *adv.* 在下面，在底下 *n.* 底部

The ring rolled underneath the sofa.

戒指滾到沙發下面了。

10 soften　[ˋsɔfn]　*vt.*　使變軟　*vi.*　變柔和

Indolent living will soften people.

生活安逸會使人們的意志消沉。

soften up 軟化

softening of the brain 癡呆

11 deepen　[ˋdipən]　*vt.*　加深　*vi.*　深化

Polishing will deepen the color of the paint.

拋光會深化油漆的顏色。

12 speckle　[ˋspɛk!]　*vt.*　使弄上斑點；沾汙　*n.*　斑點

The ring was speckled with diamonds.

戒指鑲滿了鑽石。

The bird is blue with yellow speckles.

這隻鳥是有著藍和黃色斑點。

speckles 無瑕疵的

13 enamel　[ɪˋnæm!]　*n.*　琺瑯，瓷釉　*vt.*　塗瓷釉

Some of the enamel on this pan is chipped off.

這平底鍋上的搪瓷有些已脫落。

14 lipstick　[ˋlɪp͵stɪk]　*n.*　唇膏，口紅

Lipstick and hair conditioner are cosmetics.

口紅和護髮素都是化妝品。

She put more lipstick on when she got out of the pool.

當她離開了游泳池後抹上更多的口紅。

apply lipstick 抹口紅

15 lip [lɪp] *n.* 嘴唇

He kissed her on the lips.

他吻了她的嘴唇。

lip gloss 唇彩

16 perfume [pɚˋfjum] *n.* 香水，芳香；香料

I'll always remember the smell of her perfume.

我會永遠記得她的香水味。

perfumed talk 壞話

17 fragrance [ˋfregrəns] *n.* 香味

The fragrance always reminds me of springtime at home.

這香味讓我想起了家鄉的春天。

主題 3

18 smelt [smɛlt] *v.* 熔解，熔煉；聞

Her hair smelt fragrant.

她的頭髮聞起來很香。

smelt atrocious 聞起來很噁心

smell a rat 感到不妙

smell out 查出

19 vapor [ˋvepɚ] *n.* 蒸汽 *vt.* 使蒸發 *vi.* 汽化

Water vapor condensed on the windows and made vision difficult.

水蒸氣凝結在窗戶上讓視野很差。

The rain vaporized in the desert heat.

雨水在熱沙漠蒸發。

20 bouquet　[buˋke]　*n.*　花束

He bought a bouquet at the florist.

他在花店買了一束花。

21 rose　[roz]　*n.*　玫瑰花

The rose represents England.

玫瑰花是英格蘭的象徵。

22 maiden　[ˋmedn]　*n.*　少女，未婚女子　*adj.*　未婚的

The maiden was the most beautiful girl I'd ever seen.

這少女是我見過的最漂亮的姑娘。

23 lass　[læs]　*n.*　少女，愛人，情婦

She is a bonny lass.

她是一個美麗的少女。

The lass is free and innocent.

這少女無憂無慮。

24 chaste　[tʃest]　*adj.*　貞潔的，樸實的

She had a pure, chaste view on the world.

她對世界有純真無邪的看法。

remain chaste 保持純潔

chasteness 貞操

25 youthful　[ˋjuθfəl]　*adj.*　年輕的，青年的

He had a youthful, optimistic outlook on the world.

他有年輕、樂觀的世界展望。

26 complexion [kəm`plɛkʃən] *n.* 膚色，局面 *vt.* 使增添色彩

That color doesn't suit your complexion.
那顏色不適合你的膚色。

Her complexion was a perfect light brown.
她的膚色是一個完美的淺棕色。

27 exceedingly [ɪk`sidɪŋlɪ] *adv.* 極端地，非常

That guy is an exceedingly tedious fellow.
那男人是一個非常令人生厭的傢伙。

exceedingly difficult 極難

主題 3

28 heavenly [`hɛvənlɪ] *adj.* 天堂般的，神聖的 *adv.* 無比

We spent a heavenly day at the beach.
我們在海濱痛痛快快地玩了一天。

29 godlike [`gɑd,laɪk] *adj.* 神似的，莊嚴的，與神相稱的

He had a godlike reputation in popular culture.
他在流行文化中有著神聖的聲譽。

30 goddess [`gɑdɪs] *n.* 女神；絕世美女

That model is beautiful. She's simply a goddess.
那個模特兒很漂亮。她根本是位絕世美女。

Unit **10**

Accessories 配件

 Track 34

1 slipper [ˋslɪpɚ] *n.* 拖鞋，便鞋

Dad's slippers were well-worn but comfortable.

爸爸的拖鞋破舊但舒適。

2 moccasin [ˋmɑkəsn] *n.* 鹿皮鞋，軟拖鞋

Leather moccasins were first worn by American Indians.

鹿皮鞋最先被美洲印第安人穿。

3 cane [ken] *n.* 手杖；甘蔗；藤條 *vt.* 挨打

The cane made her mobile again.

手杖讓她可以再次走動。

cane chair 藤椅

cane field 甘蔗園

4 purse [pɝs] *n.* 錢包，小錢袋，手袋 *vt. vi.* 噘起

She carried her purse in her handbag.

她手提包裡帶著錢包。

purse pride 富裕引起的傲慢

5 robe [rob] *n.* 長袍；上衣 *vt.* 使穿上禮服

Grandma got up and put on her robe, then made breakfast

for us.

奶奶起床後穿上她的外袍，然後做早餐給我們。

6 **handkerchief** [ˋhæŋkɚ͵tʃɪf] *n.* 手帕

He lost his handkerchief.

他遺失了他的手帕。

handkerchief-head 在田裡幹活的人

7 **cravat** [krəˋvæt] *n.* 領巾，領結

She's wearing a polka dot cravat.

她穿著圓點領巾。

a silk cravat 絲綢領巾

8 **necklace** [ˋnɛklɪs] *n.* 項鍊，項圈

That diamond necklace is worth a lot of money.

這條鑽石項鍊是值得很多錢。

a pearl necklace 珍珠項鍊

necklet 小首飾

9 **sash** [sæʃ] *n.* 腰帶，肩帶 *vt.* 給…繫上腰帶

Girl Scouts wear badges on their sashes.

女童子軍在他們的彩帶上佩戴徽章。

10 **garland** [ˋgɑrlənd] *n.* （作為勝利標誌的）花環，獎品 *vt.* 給…戴上花環

Mom put up a garland when she decorated the house for Christmas.

主題 3

媽媽放上花環為耶誕節裝飾房子。

11 **bracelet**　[ˋbreslɪt]　*n.*　手鐲

Her bracelet is made of sliver and emeralds.

她的手鐲是由銀和翡翠做的。

12 **goody**　[ˋgʊdɪ]　*n.*　吸引人的東西；糖果；身份低微之老婦

Mom made cookies and other goodies when we came home.

我們回家時媽媽在做的餅乾和其他好吃的東西。

She had lots of little goodies hanging from her bracelet.

她的手鐲有掛許多很炫的小東西。

goody-goody 偽善的人

13 **numerous**　[ˋnjumərəs]　*adj.*　為數眾多的；許多

There were numerous people there, including the president.

那裡有成千上萬的人，包括總統在內。

14 **tinkle**　[ˋtɪŋk!]　*n.*　叮噹聲　*vt.*　使發叮噹聲　*vi.*　發鈴鈴聲

The bracelets on her wrists tinkled when she walked.

她走路時，她手腕上的手鐲叮叮噹噹的。

15 **spangle**　[ˋspæŋg!]　*n.*　（縫在衣服上的）金屬亮片，　*vt.*　使閃爍發光　*vi.*　閃爍發光

The sunlight spangled the water.

陽光下閃爍的水。

16 dazzle　　[`dæz!]　　*vt.*　　使炫耀；使迷惑　　*n.*　　耀眼的光

The diamond dazzled her.

鑽石使她眼花了。

dazzling beauty 令人眼花撩亂的美

17 super　　[`supɚ]　　*adj.*　　極好的，超級的

That was very fun; what a super game.

那是非常好玩；多麼棒的遊戲！

18 becoming　　[bɪ`kʌmɪŋ]　　*adj.*　　合適的，適當的

That dress is very becoming on you.

那件衣服十分適合你。

His manners are very becoming.

他的舉止都非常得體。

主題 3

19 feminine　　[`fɛmənɪn]　　*adj.*　　女性的；女子氣的

She is a very feminine girl.

她是一個非常女性化的女孩。

She has a lot of feminine grace and charm.

她有很多女性的優雅和魅力。

20 suitable　　[`sutəb!]　　*adj.*　　合適的；適宜的

These films are suitable for adults and children.

這些電影大人小孩皆適宜觀賞。

suitable for 適合⋯的

suitable to the occasion 切合時宜

21 **seventeen** [ˌsɛvnˋtin] *n.* 十七，十七個

I will be seventeen next birthday.

再過一次生日，我就十七歲了。

She was just seventeen.

她那時只是十七歲。

22 **subtle** [ˋsʌt!] *adj.* 微妙的；精巧的

His management style is subtle yet effective.

他的管理風格是微妙而有效的。

The perfume has a subtle hint of pear blossoms.

香水有淡淡的梨花味。

23 **effectual** [ɪˋfɛktʃʊəl] *adj.* 有效果的，有力的

His motivational methods were quite effectual.

他激勵方式是相當有效的。

Aspirin is an effectual treatment for heart attack.

阿斯匹靈是有效治療心臟病發作。

24 **shade** [ʃed] *n.* （色彩的）濃淡，深淺 *vt.* 遮蔽 *vi.* 逐漸變化

The tree gave off welcome shade in the hot sun.

在炎炎烈日下，樹給了我們樹蔭。

Her lipstick was a light shade of pink.

她的口紅是個淡淡的粉紅色。

25 don [dɑn] *v.* 穿衣，戴帽

He donned a wet suit and went surfing.

他穿上潛水衣去衝浪。

26 cape [kep] *n.* 披肩，斗篷；海角

Red Riding Hood always wore her cape.

小紅帽總是穿著她的披肩。

27 sable [`seb!] *n.* 黑貂 *adj.* 黑色的

Sable is my favorite kind of fur.

貂毛是我最喜歡種毛皮。

a sable coat 紫貂皮短大衣

28 regal [`rig!] *adj.* 帝王的，華麗的

The regal lady impressed him.

那位雍容華貴的婦人使他印象深刻。

regal title 王的稱號

regal banquet 豪華的宴會

29 excellence [`ɛks!əns] *n.* 優秀，卓越，優點

He showed excellence throughout his school career.

他在學校生涯中表現卓越。

30 visible [`vɪzəb!] *adj.* 可見的，看得見的

The fish is visible below the surface of the river.

魚在河水下清晰可見。

主題 3

Jewelry 珠寶

Track 35

1　array　[ə`re]　*vt.*　裝扮　*n.*　佇列；排列
They are all in holiday array.
他們都穿著節日盛裝。

2　extravagant　[ɪk`strævəgənt]　*adj.*　奢侈的；過度的
The room decorations for the Christmas party were extravagant.
聖誕晚會的房間裝飾奢華。
The preparations for the wedding were extravagant.
婚禮的籌備是極盡奢華。
extravagant tastes 奢華品味
extravagantly 揮霍無度地

3　indulge　[ɪn`dʌldʒ]　*vt.*　放縱（感情）　*vi.*　縱情
He indulged his children too much.
他太縱容他的孩子們了。
indulge in 沉湎於

4 select [sə`lɛkt] *vt.* *vi.* 選擇；挑選 *adj.* 精選的

She selected a diamond ring from the collection.

她從收藏品中挑選了一枚鑽石戒指。

select society 上流社會

select a sound 選擇聲音

5 jewelry [`dʒuəlrɪ] *n.* 珠寶，珠寶飾物

My grandma has bequeathed me her jewelry.

我外婆把她的珠寶遺贈給我。

diamond jewellery 鑽石首飾

costume jewellery 人造珠寶飾物

6 gild [gɪld] *vt.* 鍍金，虛飾，裝飾

He bought his mom a gilt brooch.

他給他媽媽買了一枚鍍金胸針。

gild the lily 畫蛇添足

7 polish [`pɑlɪʃ] *vt.* 磨光；使優美

The diamonds were polished to a dazzling brilliance.

鑽石被拋光到耀眼的光彩。

8 luster [`lʌstɚ] *n.* 光彩，榮譽，光澤

The luster of the diamond ring was almost blinding.

鑽戒的光澤幾乎讓人眩目。

【反】lusterless

主題 3

9　gleam　　[glim]　*n.*　微光　*vi.*　發微光

The house gleamed when she finished cleaning.

當她打掃完房子閃閃發光。

The gleaming car made him smile.

閃閃發光的車讓他微笑。

10　glitter　　[ˋglɪtɚ]　*vi.*　閃閃發光　*n.*　閃光

All that glitters is not gold.

【諺】閃閃發光的都不是金子。

11　golden　　[ˋgoldn]　*adj.*　金（黃）色的

Speech is silver; silence is golden.

【諺】雄辯是銀，沉默是金。

12　pure　　[pjʊr]　*adj.*　純粹的；純潔的

She is a pure girl.

她是一個純潔的女孩。

She speaks pure English.

她說純正的英語。

13　luxurious　　[lʌgˋʒʊrɪəs]　*adj.*　愛好奢侈的，豪華的

The room was decorated with luxurious furnishings.

房間裝飾著豪華的家具。

14　dignify　　[ˋdɪgnə͵faɪ]　*vt.*　增威嚴，使高貴，故作顯貴

He felt that his formal suit would help dignify the occasion.

他認為這種正式的西裝將有助於顯貴場合。

15 crown [kraʊn] *n.* 王冠，冕；花冠 *vt.* 為…加冠

She won the crown in 1990.

她於 1990 年獲得冠軍。

crown all 涵蓋一切，錦上添花

16 gem [dʒɛm] *n.* 寶石，珠寶

The price of this gem is astronomical.

這個寶石的價格是個天文數位。

gem-pure 非常清晰的

gem-studded 鑲滿寶石的

17 jewel [`dʒuəl] *n.* 寶石；寶石飾物 *vt.* 用寶石裝飾

A jewel fell off my aunt's necklace, and she could find neither hide nor hair of it.

一顆寶石從我姑姑的項鍊上脫落了，她四下找，卻杳無蹤跡。

jewel-like 貴重的

主題 3

18 diamond [`daɪəmənd] *n.* 金剛石，鑽石；菱形

The diamond engagement ring made her smile broadly.

鑽石訂婚戒指讓她笑咪咪。

a diamond of 10 grams 10 克的鑽石

19 ruby [`rubɪ] *n.* 紅寶石 *adj.* 紅寶石色的 *vt.* 把…染成紅寶石色

The ruby sets off her skin.

紅寶石把她的肌膚襯托得更美麗。

ruby port 深紅色葡萄酒

20 emerald [ˋɛmərəld] *n.* 祖母綠，翡翠 *adj.* 翠綠色的

My mom wears a ring set with emeralds on her right hand.

我媽右手上戴著一枚鑲有綠寶石的戒指。

emerald green 鮮綠色

emerald wedding 翠玉婚

21 pearl [pɝl] *n.* 珍珠；珍珠母 *vt.* 用珍珠裝飾 *vi.* 採珍珠

The chain bracelet is made of natural pearls.

這手鍊是由天然珍珠做成的。

pearl eye 魚眼；白內障

pearl blue 淺藍灰色

22 treasure [ˋtrɛʒɚ] *n.* 財富；財寶 *vt.* 珍視

The men buried their treasure deep in the sand.

那些人把他們的財寶深深地埋在沙子裡。

23 collection [kəˋlɛkʃən] *n.* 搜集，收集；收藏品

The book has pride of place in her collection.

這本書在她的收藏品中最為珍貴。

collection agency 為其他公司代收欠款的公司

collection item 支票存款

24 delicate [ˋdɛləkət] *adj.* 纖細的；易碎的

The eye operation was a very delicate procedure.

眼科手術是一個非常棘手的的過程。

delicate feelings 細膩的感情

25 wondrous　　[ˋwʌndrəs]　*adj.*　令人驚奇的，非常的

The museum featured a display of wondrous stones.

博物館的特色展示一個奇妙的石頭。

26 sumptuous　　[ˋsʌmptʃʊəs]　*adj.*　豪華的，奢侈的，華麗的

The club furnishings were expensive and sumptuous.

這個俱樂部家具昂貴且奢華。

sumptuous furnishings 奢華的室內陳設

27 beauteous　　[ˋbjutɪəs]　*adj.*　美麗的

The mountain valley is a beauteous place.

山谷是一個美麗的地方。

28 matchless　　[ˋmætʃlɪs]　*adj.*　無敵的，無比的

His motorcycle collection is matchless in size and scope.

他的摩托車收藏是無與倫比的規模和範圍。

a woman of matchless beauty 天姿國色

29 inheritance　　[ɪnˋhɛrɪtəns]　*n.*　遺傳，遺產

His inheritance was enough to pay for his education.

他的遺產足以支付他的教育。

30 posterity　　[pɑsˋtɛrətɪ]　*n.*　後代，子孫

I'm leaving all my wealth to posterity.

我留下我所有的財富都給子孫。

Gossip 八卦

 Track 36

1 **teenager** [ˋtin͵edʒɚ] *n.* 青少年

He is a teenager who likes to play computer games in his free time.

他是個少年人，喜歡在空閒時間玩電腦遊戲。

2 **discord** [ˋdɪskɔrd] *n.* 爭吵，不和

She's been a source of discord and worry.

她成為不合與煩惱的根源。

apple of discord 爭端；禍根

3 **jealousy** [ˋdʒɛləsɪ] *n.* 妒忌，嫉妒，猜忌

Can I assign jealousy as the motive for the crime?

我能否確定這一犯罪動機是出於嫉妒？

jealous of 妒忌

4 **enmity** [ˋɛnmətɪ] *n.* 敵意，仇恨

His enmity toward his boss was very apparent.

他的老闆對他的敵意是非常明顯的。

5 **hostile** [ˋhɑstɪl] *adj.* 敵方的；不友善的

I don't know why he is hostile to you.

我不知道他為什麼對你抱有敵意。

hostile attitude 敵對的態度

hostile merger 惡意合併

hostile takeover 惡性接收

6 malice [`mælɪs] *n.* 惡意；蓄意犯罪

There was a smack of malice in his last letter.

在他最後的一封信中含有惡意。

7 inflame [ɪn`flem] *vt.* 使燃燒，激怒（某人） *vi.* 著火

He was inflamed with anger.

他滿腔怒火。

inflamed tissue 發炎組織

主題 3

8 shrill [ʃrɪl] *adj.* 尖聲的 *vt.* 尖聲地叫 *vi.* 發尖銳刺耳的聲音

The call of that bird is quite shrill.

那隻鳥的是很叫聲很刺耳。

9 brutal [`brut!] *adj.* 殘忍的，嚴酷的

The army was brutal in their treatment of captured civilians.

軍隊在殘酷對待被俘的平民。

brutalism 野獸派藝術

brutalization 殘酷

10 indignant [ɪn`dɪgnənt] *adj.* 憤慨的，義憤的

She is indignant at the false accusation.

她對被誣告憤憤不平。

filled with indignation 義憤填膺

【同】angry, furious, resentful

11 **fume** [fjum] *n.* *vt.* 憤怒，冒煙 *vt.* 發怒 *n.* （有害的）煙，氣

She fumed at the delay.

她對耽擱感到憤怒。

fume over sth. 為某事發怒

12 **damn** [dæm] *vt.* 詛咒 *n.* 詛咒；絲毫

The book was damned by the critics.

這本書受到批評家的指責。

13 **denounce** [dɪ`naʊns] *vt.* 譴責，聲討；告發

He denounced his critics, telling them they had the facts wrong.

他譴責批評他的人，告訴他們是他們把事實搞錯了。

denounce an accusation 譴責指控

14 **falsehood** [`fɔls,hʊd] *n.* 謊言，虛假

He is famous for his elaborate falsehoods.

他善於精心的謊言。

false face 假面具

falsehood 謬誤，不真實

15 **contemptible** [kən`tɛmptəb!] *adj.* 令人輕視的

His deed is contemptible.

他的行為是可輕視的。

contemptible behavior 卑鄙的行為

a contemptible lie 無恥的謊言

16 **wanton** [ˋwɑntən] *adj.* 頑皮的，放縱的 *vt.* 揮霍 *vi.* 任性

The yard was left to a wanton growth of weeds.

庭院裡雜草叢生。

wanton disregard 肆意妄為

17 **cowardly** [ˋkaʊədlɪ] *adj.* 懦弱的，卑怯的 *adv.* 膽小地

It is cowardly of her not to admit her mistake.

她不承認錯誤就不是好樣兒。

主題 3

18 **brazen** [ˋbrezən] *adj.* 無恥的，厚臉皮的 *vt.* 厚著臉皮做

It was brazen of him to say so!

他這樣說真是無恥！

brazen out 厚著臉對待

brazen-faced 臉皮厚的

19 **lament** [ləˋmɛnt] *n.* *vt.* *vi.* 悲傷、哀悼 *n.* 悲痛之情；哀歌

He deeply lamented the death of his daughter.

他對女兒的逝世深感悲痛。

lament over 哀悼

lamentable 不快的

20 **lamentation** [ˌlæmənˈteʃən] *n.* 悲歎，哀悼；慟哭

It was a time for lamentation.

這是一個悼念的時刻。

lamentations of sorrow 悲嘆的悲哀

21 **observe** [əbˈzɝv] *vt.* 看到，注意到 *vi.* 觀察

"You see, but you do not observe," said Holmes.

「你有看，但沒在觀察。」福爾摩斯說。

observe on 評論

22 **tease** [tiz] *vt.* 逗樂，戲弄；強求 *vi.* 取笑 *n.* 愛戲弄人的人

His sister liked to tease him when he was trying to relax.

當他試圖休息時，他的姐姐喜歡戲弄他。

23 **flirt** [flɝt] *vi.* 不認真考慮，調戲，挑逗 *vt.* 輕快地擺動 *n.* 調情者

The guy is a terrible flirt.

那男人是調情色鬼。

flirt with sb. 與調情某人

24 **rumor** [ˈrumɚ] *n.* 謠言，謠傳，傳聞 *vt.* 謠傳

Do not worry about the rumor.

別擔心謠言。

25 harmless [ˋhɑrmlɪs] *adj.* 無害的

This snake is harmless.

這條蛇是無毒的。

26 trifle [ˋtraɪf!] *vi.* 閑混；嬉耍 *vt.* 浪費 *n.* 小事；少量

That problem is but a trifle in the bigger picture.

這個問題只不過是在大局觀中的小事。

trifle away 浪費

trifle with 視同兒戲

27 folly [ˋfɑlɪ] *n.* 愚蠢

Beauty and folly are often companions.

【諺】美貌和愚蠢常結伴。

主題 **3**

28 genial [ˋdʒinjəl] *adj.* 愉快的，脾氣好的

The waitress' genial smile made me feel at home.

女服務生親切的笑容使我感覺賓至如歸。

genial companion 親切的伴侶

29 meekness [ˋmiknɪs] *n.* 溫順，柔和

Meekness is one of her virtues.

溫順是她的優點之一。

meek-eyed 目光柔和的

30 congenial [kənˋdʒinjəl] *adj.* 意氣相投的，友善的

They are of a congenial temper.

他們的性情相投。

主題 4

Food & Health

食物與健康

Vegetables 蔬菜

Track 37

1 plot [hæt] *n.* 小塊土地 *vt.* 密謀

Morris grows vegetables on his little plot of land.

Morris 在他的小土地上種蔬菜。

2 plant [plænt] *n.* 植物；工廠 *vt.* 栽種

He works at a power plant.

他在發電廠工作。

Plants need water and sunshine.

植物需要水和陽光。

Tree Planting Day 植樹節

3 sow [so] *vt.* 播（種） *vi.* 播種

The farmer sowed the field with corn.

那個農夫在田地耕種。

關於 "farming" 還有以下片語 : plow a field, sow seeds, spread manure, water crops, thresh grain。

4 reap [rip] *vt.* *vi.* 收割，收穫

You reap what you sow.

【諺】一分耕耘，一分收獲。

【同】harvest

5 herb [hɝb] *n.* 草本植物；香草

The doctor alighted on a rare medical herb.
醫生偶然找到了一種稀有的草藥。
herbal *adj.* 草本的
herbal medicine 草藥

6 beet [bit] *n.* 甜菜

Beets are my sister's favorite food.
甜菜根是我妹妹最喜歡的食物。

7 bean [bin] *n.* 豆，蠶豆

A bean grows rapidly.
豆類植物生長很快。
lima beans 青豆
jelly beans 軟心豆粒糖

8 tomato [tə`meto] *n.* 蕃茄

Would you like some tomato juice?
你想要些番茄汁嗎？
sliced tomatoes 切片蕃茄
tomato juice 蕃茄汁
蕃茄醬是用 tomato 做的，但是英文是 ketchup / catsup。

主題 4

9 lettuce [`lɛtɪs] *n.* 萵苣

I need you to buy a couple heads of lettuce.
我需要你買兩個萵苣。
a bacon, lettuce sandwich 一個培根萵苣三明治

10 cabbage　[ˋkæbɪdʒ]　*n.*　高麗菜，捲心菜

The farmer is busy picking out cabbage seedlings.

農夫正忙著挑選出高麗菜苗。

grow cabbages 種植高麗菜

11 celery　[ˋsɛlərɪ]　*n.*　芹菜

She has a thing about celery.

她很討厭芹菜。

12 salad　[ˋsæləd]　*n.*　沙拉；萵苣，生菜

I am fond of potato salad.

我喜歡馬鈴薯沙拉。

13 root　[rut]　*n.*　根，根子　*vt.*　生根

We dug up the root of the tree.

我們挖起了這棵樹的根。

The plant roots quickly.

這種植物生根生得很快。

14 potato　[pəˋteto]　*n.*　馬鈴薯

One of my favorite foods is potato.

馬鈴薯是我最愛的食物之一。

mashed potatoes 馬鈴薯泥

sweet potatoes 地瓜，山芋

15 poppy　[ˋpɑpɪ]　*n.*　罌粟，深紅色

Poppies are not allowed to be planted in some countries.

在一些國家，罌粟被禁止種植。

poppy fields 罌粟田

poppy seeds 罌粟種子

16 upward　[ˋʌpwɚd]　*adv.*　向上

The growth of the plant was sideward rather than upward.

那個植物的生長是向旁邊的而不是向上的。

an upward gaze 向上的凝視

17 pumpkin　[ˋpʌmpkɪn]　*n.*　南瓜，南瓜藤

His wife made some pumpkin pies for supper.

他妻子做了一些南瓜餡餅作晚餐。

18 pea　[pi]　*n.*　豌豆；豌豆屬植物

Would you like a bowl of pea soup?

你要不要來碗豌豆湯？

19 pickle　[ˋpɪk!]　*n.*　醃製食品，泡菜

The dish was accompanied by pickles.

這盤菜配有泡菜。

in a pickle 處於困難、不開心的狀況

20 gardener　[ˋgɑrdənɚ]　*n.*　園丁，花匠

He is a skilled gardener.

他是個厲害的園丁。

主題 4

21 flourish　[ˈflɝɪʃ]　*vi.*　繁榮，茂盛，興旺

This type of plant flourishes in tropical countries.

這種植物在熱帶國家生長茂盛。

22 artificial　[ˌɑrtəˈfɪʃəl]　*adj.*　人工的；矯揉造作的

She decorated her room with artificial flowers.

她用人造花佈置她的房間。

【同】man-made, synthetic

【反】natural

23 buckwheat　[ˈbʌkˌhwit]　*n.*　蕎麥，蕎麥之種，蕎麥粉

They planted some buckwheat in the fields.

他們在田裡種蕎麥。

24 chew　[tʃu]　*vt.*　咀嚼，嚼碎

Grandmother can't chew without her false teeth.

奶奶沒有假牙就嚼不動。

【同】gnaw, crunch

25 planter　[ˈplæntɚ]　*n.*　種植者，耕作者，殖民者

His brother is a tea planter.

他的哥哥是一個茶園主。

26 plantation　[plænˈteʃən]　*n.*　種植園；栽植

There were hundreds of slaves on the plantation.

這個種植園裡有數百名奴隸。

27 ripen　　[`raɪpən]　*vt.*　使熟　*vi.*　成熟

The corn ripens in the sun.

農作物在陽光下成熟。

ripeness　*n.*　成熟

28 wilt　　[wɪlt]　*v.*　使……凋謝，枯萎

The flowers are wilting for lack of water.

這些花因缺水而漸漸枯萎。

【同】droop

29 blight　　[blaɪt]　*n.*　植物枯萎病　*v.*　使……枯萎

Her life was blighted by ill health.

她的一生被疾病所摧殘。

【反】wither, destroy

30 trample　　[`træmp!]　*vt.*　*vi.*　*n.*　踐踏，蹂躪

Don't trample the grass.

不要踐踏草地。

【同】tread, stamp, crush, squash

主題 4

Unit
02

Fruit 水果

Track 38

1 **fruit** [frut] *n.* 水果

An apple is a kind of fruit.
蘋果是一種水果。
a lot of fruit 許多水果
bear fruit 結果；產生效果

2 **seed** [sid] *n.* 種子

The farmers were scattering seed on the fields.
農夫把種子撒在田裡。

3 **blossom** [`blɑsəm] *n.* 花；開花 *vi.* 開花

The apple trees are in blossom.
蘋果樹正在開花。
cherry blossom 櫻花

4 **fragrant** [`fregrənt] *adj.* 香的；芬芳的

The herb gave off a fragrant odor.
香草發出一陣幽香。
fragrant oil 精油

5 **apple** [ˋæp!] *n.* 蘋果

An apple a day keeps the doctor away.

【諺】一日一蘋果，醫生遠離我。

pick apples 摘蘋果

the apple of sb.'s eye 情人眼中之最愛

6 **pie** [paɪ] *n.* （西點）餡餅

Help yourself to this meat pie.

請吃點肉派。

a meat pie 肉餅

a fruit pie 水果派

as easy as pie 很簡單

7 **melon** [ˋmɛlən] *n.* 瓜；甜瓜

The little boy picked a melon from the field.

小男孩從田裡摘了一顆甜瓜。

honey melon 香瓜

watermelon 西瓜

主題 4

8 **coconut** [ˋkokəˌnət] *n.* 椰子

My mom split open the coconut.

我媽媽把椰子剖開。

9 **pick**　[pɪk]　*v.*　採摘　*n.*　選擇

He picked her a rose.

他採了一朵玫瑰給她。

pick out 挑選

pick up 拾起，搭載，摘

pick and choose 挑挑揀揀

pick a fight 主動引起爭端

10 **juice**　[dʒus]　*n.*　（水果等）汁；液

I like to drink coconut juice.

我喜歡喝椰子汁。

let someone stew in their own juice 讓某人自食惡果

11 **banana**　[bəˋnænə]　*n.*　香蕉

I gave Mary an apple in exchange for my banana.

我給瑪麗一個蘋果換我最喜歡吃的香蕉。

a bunch of bananas 一串香蕉

a hand of bananas 一串香蕉

12 **peel**　[pil]　*vt.*　剝（皮）；削（皮）

His job was to peel potatoes.

他的工作是削馬鈴薯皮。

13 **grape**　[grep]　*n.*　葡萄；葡萄藤

Red wine is made from grapes.

紅酒是用葡萄做成的。

14 orange [ˋɔrɪndʒ] *n.* 柳丁

Would you like some orange juice?

你想要來些柳橙汁嗎？

orange peel 柳丁皮

15 abundant [əˋbʌndənt] *adj.* 豐富的；大量的

The Middle East is abundant in petroleum deposits.

中東的石油蘊藏量豐富。

16 scanty [ˋskæntɪ] *adj.* 缺乏的；僅有的；節省的；狹小的

He is scanty with words.

他沉默寡言。

【同】deficient, destitute, devoid

【反】abundant, sufficient, profuse

17 copious [ˋkopɪəs] *adj.* 豐富的；多產的

She was a copious writer.

她是位作品數量多的作家。

copiously *adv.* 豐富地，充裕地

copiousness *n.* 豐裕，大量

【同】plentiful, abundant

18 soil [sɔɪl] *n.* 土壤；土地

Fertile soil yields good crops.

肥沃的土地能種出好莊稼。

stop the soil getting too dry 阻止土壤變得太乾

hold the soil in place 保持那個地方的土壤

主題 **4**

19 nourishment   [`nɝɪʃmənt]   *n.*   食物；營養（情況）

Plants get nourishment from the soil.

植物從土壤中吸取養料。

lack of proper nourishment 缺乏適當的營養

20 pear   [pɛr]   *n.*   梨

The branch of the pear tree is weighed down heavily with fruits.

梨樹的樹枝給沉甸甸的果實壓彎了。

two pears 兩個梨

21 berry   [`bɛrɪ]   *n.*   漿果（如草莓等）

This jam is made of berries.

這個果醬是由漿果做成的。

22 currant   [`kɝ-ənt]   *n.*   葡萄乾

We have currant buns for afternoon tea.

我們的下午茶有葡萄乾小圓麵包。

23 handful   [`hændfəl]   *n.*   一把；少數；一小撮

I put a handful of coins in my pocket.

我在口袋裡放了一把硬幣。

【同】few, several

24 sweetness   [`switnɪs]   *n.*   甜蜜；新鮮；溫和

They finally can enjoy the sweetness of freedom.

他們終於可以享受自由的快樂。

25 indulgence　[ɪnˋdʌldʒəns]　*n.*　沉溺；放縱；嗜好

Reading is my only indulgence.

閱讀是我唯一的嗜好。

26 bloom　[blum]　*vi.*　開花　*n.*　花；開花

The roses are blooming.

玫瑰花正在盛開。

27 manure　[məˋnjʊr]　*n.*　肥料；糞肥

Animal dung may be used as manure.

動物的糞便可以作為肥料使用。

28 fertilizer　[ˋfɝtl͵aɪzɚ]　*n.*　肥料

Get some more fertilizer for the garden.

給花園再多施些肥料。

29 ripen　[ˋraɪpən]　*vt.*　使熟　*vi.*　成熟

The crops ripen in the sun.

農作物在陽光下成熟。

主題 4

30 ripe　[raɪp]　*adj.*　熟的；時機成熟的

He is ripe in judgment.

他的判斷很成熟。

The time is ripe for taking action.

採取行動的時間已經成熟了。

Meals 餐

 Track 39

1 meal [mil] *n.* （一）餐，（一頓）飯食

I had a solid meal.

我飽餐了一頓。

light meal 便飯

midday meal 午飯

2 starve [starv] *vi.* 餓死 *vt.* 使餓死

Many children starved to death in Africa.

很多在非洲的小孩餓死了。

starve for 渴望得到

starve to death 餓死

3 eat [it] *vt.* 吃，喝 *vi.* 吃飯

Where shall we eat today?

今天我們去哪裡吃飯？

eat up 吃完，吃光

eat to live 為活而吃

4 breakfast [ˋbrɛkfəst] *n.* 早飯，早餐

We were having breakfast.

我們正在吃早餐。

have breakfast 吃早飯

at breakfast 早餐時、正吃早餐

5 toast [tost] *n.* 烤麵包 *vt.* 烘，烤

The little girl spread some chocolate jam on her toast.

小女孩把巧克力醬塗在她吐司上。

【同】drink, pledge, tribute

6 egg [ɛg] *n.* 蛋

Do you want a boiled egg for breakfast?

你早餐飯要吃煮雞蛋嗎？

a boiled egg 煮熟的蛋

ham and eggs 火腿蛋

7 sandwich [ˋsændwɪtʃ] *vt.* 夾入，擠進

I sandwiched the cakes together with some cream.

我把蛋糕兩塊餅夾些奶油做成三明治。

8 bread [brɛd] *n.* 麵包

The bread is baking in the oven.

烤箱裡正在烤麵包。

a piece (slice) of bread 一片麵包

a loaf of bread 一條麵包

9 lunch [lʌntʃ] *n.* 午餐，(美) 便餐

We had an awful lunch.

我們吃了頓很糟的午餐。

have a light lunch 吃清淡的午餐

a lunch box 便當盒

10 luncheon [ˋlʌntʃən] *n.* 午宴，午餐，便宴

I have our new partner to the luncheon tomorrow.

我明天請我們的新夥伴吃午飯。

11 noon [nun] *n.* 中午，正午

It's my grandpa's habit to take a nap at noon.

我爺爺有睡午覺的習慣。

We have lunch at noon.

我們中午在正午吃午飯。

at noon 在中午

12 supper [ˋsʌpɚ] *n.* 晚餐

What did you have for supper?

你晚餐吃什麼？

have supper 吃晚餐

have rice for supper 晚飯吃米飯

13 night [naɪt] *n.* 夜，夜間

We can see the stars at night.

夜晚我們可以看見星群。

at night 夜間，晚上

in the night 晚上

14 main [men] *adj.* 主要的 *n.* 主要部分

Our main meal is in the evening.

我們主要的那餐是在晚上。

note down the main points of the speech 記下講演的重點

15 cheese [tʃiz] *n.* 乳酪，乾酪

She doesn't like the smell of this cheese.

她不喜歡這塊乳酪的味道。

16 dairy [`dɛrɪ] *n.* 牛奶場；乳製品

We buy milk and butter at the dairy.

我們在牛奶場買了牛奶和奶油。

17 nourish [`nɝɪʃ] *vt.* 提供養分，養育

Milk is all we need to nourish a small baby.

我們供給嬰兒營養只需餵奶就夠了。

主題 4

18 nourishment [`nɝɪʃmənt] *n.* 食物；營養（情況）

Plants get nourishment from the soil.

植物從土壤中吸取養料。

19 digestion [də`dʒɛstʃən] *n.* 消化

Porridge is good for your digestion.

粥有益於消化。

20 rice [raɪs] *n.* 米飯；大米

Rice is an essential foodstuff in Asia.
大米是我們生活的基本食物。
a bowl of rice 一碗米飯
grow rice 種水稻

21 bowl [bol] *n.* 碗

I have a bowl of cereal every morning.
我每天早晨吃一碗麥片粥。
two bowls of boiled rice 兩碗米飯

22 soup [sup] *n.* 湯

A bowl of hot chicken soup is good for you.
喝一碗熱雞湯對你有好處。
eat soup for breakfast 早飯喝湯
a bowl of soup 一碗湯

23 buffet [`bʌfɪt] *n.* 自助餐，小賣部，沖擊，毆打，碗櫥

We had a buffet supper last week.
我們上禮拜吃了了一次自助晚餐。
【同】cafeteria

24 yourselves [jur`sɛlvz] *pron.* 你們自己

Help yourselves to some sandwiches.
請你們自己隨意拿三明治吃。

25 **homely** [ˋhomlɪ] *adj.* 家庭的；家常的

They had a homely meal of bread and milk.

他們吃了頓麵包加牛奶的家常便餐。

26 **appetite** [ˋæpə,taɪt] *n.* 食欲，胃口；欲望

The long work gave her a good appetite.

長時間工作使她食慾旺盛。

27 **gobble** [ˋgɑb!] *v.* 貪婪地吃，吞沒

She gobbled up all the relevant books.

她如饑似渴地收集一切有關的書籍。

28 **swallow** [ˋswɑlo] *n.* *vt.* *vi.* 吞，咽

He swallowed her bitterness and carried on.

他忍氣吞聲地繼續進下去。

29 **full** [fʊl] *adj.* 滿

The bottle is full of water.

瓶子裡裝滿了水。

have a full meal 飽餐一頓

get a full mark 得滿分

30 **relish** [ˋrɛlɪʃ] *n.* *v.* 味道，喜好，享受

The professor had no relish for his jokes.

那位教授對他的笑話不感興趣。

主題 4

Meat 肉

Track 40

1 **red** [rɛd] *adj.* 紅色的

The sky changed from blue to red.

天空由藍色變為紅色。

red flag 紅旗

red ink 紅墨水

2 **white** [hwaɪt] *adj.* 白色的

This mat is white.

這塊地毯是白色的。

Her skin is as white as snow.

她的皮膚白如雪。

white-haired 白髮的

3 **food** [fud] *n.* 食物

Is he used to the food here?

他習慣吃這兒的飯菜嗎？

seafood 海產食物

clothing, food and housing 衣食住

4 manifold [`mænə,fold] *adj.* 繁多的，多種的

The uses of this coffee machine are manifold.

這台咖啡機有多種用途。

5 agriculture [`ægrɪ,kʌltʃɚ] *n.* 農業，農藝；農學

Modern industry is replacing agriculture in our once beautiful countryside.

現代工業正在破壞我們美麗的農村。

the science of agriculture 農業科學

research into agriculture 研究農業

6 poultry [`poltrɪ] *n.* 家禽

The poultry are being fed.

家禽正在吃飼料。

7 pigeon [`pɪdʒɪn] *n.* 鴿子

A pigeon is resting up in one of the pines.

一隻鴿子正在松樹上休息。

8 pig [pɪg] *n.* 豬

A pig is a domestic animal.

豬是一種家畜。

Pigs stay in the pigsty.

豬待在豬圈裡。

主題 4

9　**pork**　[pork]　*n.*　豬肉

The grease from pork can be used for frying.

豬肉煉出的油可用來煎炸食物。

10　**cow**　[kaʊ]　*n.*　母牛，奶牛

The cow has produced a calf.

這母牛生了一頭小牛。

milk the cow 擠牛奶

keep cows and sheep 養牛羊

11　**beef**　[bif]　*n.*　牛肉

Africa is exporting beef to Europe.

非洲向歐洲出口牛肉。

How about some more beef?

多來點牛肉怎麼樣？

12　**hamburger**　[ˋhæmbɝgɚ]　*n.*　漢堡包，牛肉餅

She goes there to drink a coke and eat a hamburger.

她到那裡喝一瓶可樂和吃一個漢堡。

13　**butcher**　[ˋbʊtʃɚ]　*n.*　屠夫；屠殺者

The man is a real butcher.

那個人是一個殺人魔。

the butcher's 肉鋪

14　**slaughter**　[ˋslɔtɚ]　*vt.*　&　*n.*　屠殺，屠宰

Millions of cattle are slaughtered every day.

每天有數百萬頭牛被屠殺。

【同】assassinate, butcher, kill

15 **tough**　[tʌf]　*adj.*　堅韌的；健壯的

The company faces tough competition.

這家公司面臨著艱難的競爭。

【同】difficult, hard, troublesome

【反】tender, soft, fragile, frail

16 **tender**　[ˋtɛndɚ]　*adj.*　嫩的；脆弱的

There are a lot of tender flowers in my garden.

我的花園裡盡是嬌嫩的花朵。

17 **hot**　[hɑt]　*adj.*　熱的；刺激的；辣的

The dish is too hot for me.

這道菜對我來說太辣了。

have a hot dog 吃熱狗

hot spring 溫泉

18 **sausage**　[ˋsɔsɪdʒ]　*n.*　香腸，臘腸

He loves sausage and bacon.

他喜歡香腸和培根。

19 **chicken**　[ˋtʃɪkɪn]　*n.*　雞肉；小雞

This soup tastes of chicken.

這湯裡有雞肉的味道。

have chicken for dinner 晚餐吃雞肉

主題 4

20 **fish** [fɪʃ] *n.* 魚肉；魚

The boys caught four little fishes.
男孩們捉到四條小魚。
fish farming 漁業
fresh-water fish 淡水魚

21 **sheep** [ʃip] *n.* 羊，綿羊

Can you distinguish goats from sheep?
你能辨別山羊和綿羊的不同嗎？
sheep farms 綿羊牧場

22 **wool** [wʊl] *n.* 羊毛；毛線，絨線

The kitten is playing a skein of wool.
小貓正在玩一球毛線。
be made of wool... 用毛線製作的

23 **mutton** [`mʌtn] *n.* 羊肉

Please warm up yesterday's mutton.
請把昨天的羊肉熱一下。
muttonhead 笨蛋

24 **lamb** [læm] *n.* 羔羊，小羊；羔羊肉

She is as meek as a lamb.
她像小羊一樣的溫順。

25 **boar** [bor] *n.* 公豬，野豬

He was attacked by a wild boar.

他被一頭野豬襲擊。

26 **horse** [hɔrs] *n.* 馬

I am learning to ride a horse.
我正在學習騎馬。
Soldiers ride horses in the cavalry.
騎兵在騎馬。

27 **flesh** [flɛʃ] *n.* 肉；肉體

Lions are flesh-eating animals.
獅子是肉食動物。

28 **skin** [skɪn] *n.* 皮，皮膚

He had brown skin.
他的皮膚是棕色的。

29 **dog** [dɔg] *n.* 狗

Every dog has his day.
【諺】人人皆有得意時。
I keep a dog.
我養了一條狗。

30 **fur** [fɝ] *n.* （獸類的）軟毛；皮毛

The night was cold, so the woman wore her fur coat.
晚上冷，所以那個女人穿上她的皮衣。
expensive fur 昂貴的皮衣

Snacks 點心

 Track 41

1 between [bɪˋtwin] *prep.* 在…（兩者）之間

She is a girl between twenty and thirty.

她是個年齡在 20 到 30 歲間的女孩。

2 hungry [ˋhʌŋgrɪ] *adj.* 饑餓的；渴望的

She is hungry for the news of her son studying abroad.

她渴望得到在國外唸書的兒子的消息。

be hungry for sth. 渴求某東西

go hungry 挨餓

3 hunger [ˋhʌŋgɚ] *n.* 餓，饑餓；渴望

Hunger is a major problem in some areas of Africa.

饑餓在非洲的一些地區是個主要問題。

They all had a hunger for knowledge.

他們全都渴望知識。

4 sweet [swit] *adj.* 甜的

The apples taste sweet.

這些蘋果很甜。

sweet potato 紅薯，山芋

a sweet paper 一張糖紙

5 **candy** [`kændɪ] *n.* 糖果；砂糖結晶

His pocket was all gummed up with candy.
他的口袋全被糖粘住了。

6 **chocolate** [`tʃɑkəlɪt] *n.* 巧克力；巧克力糖

The cook covered the cakes with chocolate sprinkles.
廚師給蛋糕灑上巧克力末。
a cup of chocolate 一杯可可飲料
a box of chocolates 一盒巧克力

7 **brownie** [`braʊnɪ] *n.* 餅

The waiter served us brownies as dessert.
服務生給我們吃核桃仁巧克力餅作為甜點。

8 **variety** [və`raɪətɪ] *n.* 多樣化；種類；變種

What other ways do you know to add variety?
你知道其他增加變化的方法嗎？
many varieties of 許多種
a variety of 各種，種種

主題 4

9 **cookie** [`kʊki] *n.* 餅乾

We had cookies and coffee.
我們吃了餅乾和咖啡。

10 **biscuit** [`bɪskɪt] *n.* （英）餅乾；（美）軟餅

I caught the little girl with her fingers in the biscuit tin.
我看見小女孩的手指還在餅乾盒裡。

11 crisp　　[krɪsp]　*adj.*　脆的；捲曲的

It tastes sweet and crisp.

吃起來又甜又脆。

【同】crispy, brittle, hard

12 nibble　　[`nɪb!]　*v.*　一點點地咬，慢慢啃

The man sat and nibbled on a sandwich.

那人坐下來，慢慢地吃著三明治。

13 taste　　[test]　*vt.*　嘗；嘗到　*n.*　味覺

The medicine has a bitter taste.

這藥有苦味。

It has a sweet taste.

它有一股甜味。

14 fat　　[fæt]　*adj.*　肥胖的

If you don't get more exercise, you'll get fat.

如果你不多作運動，就會發胖。

get fat 會發胖

fat meat 肥肉

15 sugar　　[`ʃʊgɚ]　*n.*　糖

He bought his daughter a packet of sugar.

他給他女兒買了一袋糖果。

put some sugar in 放裡一些糖，加些糖

sugar-coated pills 糖衣藥片

16 honey [ˋhʌnɪ] *n.* 蜂蜜；蜜

Honey can be substituted for sugar in this recipe.

在這個食譜中，可用蜂蜜代替食糖。

17 weight [wet] *n.* 重；砝碼；重擔

He has put on weight since I last saw him.

自從我上次見到他以來，他又長胖了。

What is your weight?

你的體重是多少？

18 health [hɛlθ] *n.* 健康，健康狀況

Smoking is harmful to one's health.

吸煙對健康有害。

Health is better than wealth.

【諺】健康勝於財富。

19 cheese [tʃiz] *n.* 乳酪，乾酪

I lave a taste of this chccse!

嚐一點兒這種乳酪吧！

主題 4

20 midnight [ˋmɪd͵naɪt] *n.* 午夜（晚上十二點鐘）

It's close to midnight.

已近午夜了。

go out at midnight 半夜裡跑出去

at midnight 在半夜時（指深夜十二點）

21 **cracker** [`pık!] *n.* 鹹餅乾

I had some crackers at midnight.
我半夜吃點鹹餅乾。

22 **saucer** [bol] *n.* 茶托；淺碟

Sandra offered me tea in her best cup and saucer.
Sandra 用她最好的茶杯請我喝茶。
two bowls of boiled rice 兩碗米飯

23 **nut** [nʌt] *n.* 堅果，乾果；螺母

Cashew nuts and walnuts are both nuts.
腰果和核桃都是堅果。
gather nuts 收集堅果
a hard nut 一個難對付的人

24 **almond** [`ɑmənd] *n.* 杏樹，杏仁

He bought a jar of almond paste.
他買了一罐杏仁軟糖。

25 **convenient** [kən`vinjənt] *adj.* 便利的；近便的

I'd like to visit you whenever it's convenient.
在你方便的時候我想去拜訪你。
be convenient for sb. 對某人來說是方便的
be convenient to sb. 對某人來說方便

26 common   [ˋkɑmən]   *adj.*   普通的，一般地

Common interests bind us together.

共同的利益使我們結合在一起。

in common 相似，共同有的

27 preserve   [prɪˋzɝv]   *vt.*   保護；保存；醃漬

In the summer, large crops of fruit may be preserved by freezing or bottling.

夏天收穫的大量水果可冷藏或裝瓶裝罐加以保存。

28 pudding   [ˋpʊdɪŋ]   *n.*   布丁

Let the pudding chill for half an hour.

把布丁冰鎮半小時。

29 cake   [kek]   *n.*   蛋糕，餅，糕

He passed me one fourth of the cake.

他遞給我四分之一個蛋糕。

moon cake 月餅

a cake of ice 一塊冰

主題 4

30 diet   [ˋdaɪət]   *n.*   飲食，食物

You should eat a more high-protein diet.

你應多吃些高蛋白食物。

Unit
06

Drink 飲料

Track 42

1 drink [drɪŋk] *vt.* 飲 *vi.* 喝 *n.* 飲料

He doesn't smoke or drink.

他不抽煙也不喝酒。

drink to one's health 舉杯祝某人健康

drink to our victory 舉杯慶祝我們的勝利

2 beverage [`bɛvərɪdʒ] *n.* （水，酒等之外的）飲料

Beverages are not allowed on the bus.

公車上不准喝飲料。

3 sip [sɪp] *v.* 啜飲

I sipped at the coffee.

我啜飲咖啡。

【同】taste, drop, spoonful

4 thirsty [`θɝstɪ] *adj.* 渴的；乾燥的

He was thirsty for power.

他渴望擁有權力。

5 **thirst** [θɝst] *n.* 渴，口渴；渴望

He satisfied his thirst with a glass of water.

他喝了一杯水解渴。

6 **beer** [bɪr] *n.* 啤酒

He bought a keg of beer.

他買了一桶啤酒。

7 **pint** [paɪnt] *n.* 品脫

He ordered himself a pint of beer.

他要了一品脫啤酒。

8 **wine** [waɪn] *n.* 酒

She tried to find some wine in the pantry.

她試著在餐具室找一些酒。

a glass of wine 一杯酒

wine shop 酒

主題 **4**

9 **liquor** [ˈlɪkɚ] *n.* 酒；溶液，液劑

The liquor is 80 proof.

這種酒為標準度數的 80％。

【同】alcohol, drink

10 **alcohol** [ˈælkəˌhɔl] *n.* 酒精，乙醇

He is addicted to alcohol.

他嗜好喝酒。

11 **dozen** [ˋdʌzn] *n.* 一打，十二個

My mother bought a dozen eggs.

我媽媽買了一打雞蛋。

dozens of 數十，幾十，許多

12 **necessary** [ˋnɛsəˏsɛrɪ] *adj.* 必需的，必要的

It is absolutely necessary.

這是絕對必要的。

It's necessary to do sth. 做某事是必要的

take any necessary action

採取任何必要的行動

13 **lemonade** [ˏlɛmənˋed] *n.* 檸檬水

She drinks lemonade every day.

她每天喝檸檬水。

14 **sour** [ˋsaʊr] *adj.* 酸的；脾氣壞的

Most green fruits are sour.

大多數未熟的水果都是酸的。

【同】tart, sharp, acid, pungent

15 **bottle** [ˋbɑtl] *n.* 瓶，酒瓶；一瓶

They drank a whole bottle!

他們喝了一整瓶酒！

a bottle of wine (beer) 一瓶酒（啤酒）

an ink bottle 墨水瓶

16 **goblet**　[`gɑblɪt]　*n.*　高腳酒杯

The lady poured some wine into the goblet.

婦人向高腳酒杯裡倒了一些葡萄酒。

17 **savor**　[`sevɚ]　*n.*　滋味，氣味，食欲

The woman drank the wine slowly, savoring every drop.

那女人慢慢地喝著酒，細細品嘗著每滴酒的滋味。

18 **soft**　[sɔft]　*adj.*　軟的；柔和的

The quilt feels soft and smooth.

被子摸起來柔軟光滑。

on a soft bed 在軟床上

soft drink 不含酒精的飲料，清涼飲料

19 **soda**　[`sodə]　*n.*　碳酸鈉，純鹼；汽水

Two whisky sodas, please.

請來兩杯威士忌蘇打。

soda water 汽水

主題 4

20 **crush**　[`ʃʊgɚ]　*n.*　【英】果汁飲料

She used to drink berry crush after school.

她過去習慣放學後喝草莓汁。

21 **milk**　[mɪlk]　*vt.*　*vi.*　擠奶；出奶

She is milking the cow.

她在擠牛奶。

a glass of milk 一杯牛奶

Milky Way 銀河

22 **jug** [dʒʌg] *n.* 大壺

Pour the milk into a jug.
把牛奶灌進壺裡。

23 **natural** [ˈnætʃərəl] *adj.* 自然的

She's not our natural daughter; we adopted her when she was five.
她不是我們的親生女兒，她五歲時我們領養的。
in natural science 在自然科學裡
natural gas 天然氣

24 **juice** [dʒus] *n.* （水果等）汁，液

I like to drink coconut juice.
我喜歡喝椰子汁。
【同】liquid, fluid, liquor

25 **fresh** [frɛʃ] *adj.* 新鮮的

They buy fresh meat.
他們買新鮮肉。
fresh air 涼爽的空氣
fresh news 新的消息

26 **tea** [ti] *n.* 茶；茶葉；茶樹

We have tea at four o'clock in the afternoon.
我們在下午四點鐘喝茶。

strong tea 濃茶

black tea 紅茶

27 cup　　[kʌp]　*vt.*　使成杯形

She cupped her hand behind her ear to hear better.

她把一隻手掌緊貼在耳後以便聽得清楚些。

a coffee cup 咖啡杯

half a cup of water 半杯水

28 spill　　[spɪl]　*vt.*　使溢出　*vi.*　溢出

Coffee spilled from the cup.

咖啡從杯子裡溢了出來。

【同】overturn, upset, slop

29 coffee　　[ˋkɔfɪ]　*n.*　咖啡

He put some sugar into his coffee.

他往咖啡裡加了些糖。

black coffee 黑咖啡（不加牛奶）

white coffee 加牛奶的咖啡

30 grind　　[graɪnd]　*vt.*　磨（碎）；磨快

She is busy grinding coffee.

她忙著磨咖啡豆。

主題 4

Nutrition 營養

 Track 43

1　mortality　[mɔr`tælətɪ]　*n.*　必死的命運，死亡數目，死亡率

He was suddenly aware of his own mortality.

他突然意識到自己的死亡。

infant mortality rate 嬰兒夭折率

mortality table 死亡率表

2　vice　[vaɪs]　*n.*　罪惡；惡習；缺點

He has many vices, smoking among them.

他有很多惡習，吸煙是其中之一。

3　maybe　[`mebɪ]　*adv.*　大概，或許

Maybe these nutrients are helpful to her health.

或許這些營養品對她的健康有幫助。

maybe tomorrow 或許明天

definitely maybe 絕對可能

4　forbidden　[fɚ`bɪdn]　*adj.*　被禁止的，嚴禁的

Smoking is forbidden in the restaurant.

餐廳禁止吸菸。

expressly forbidden 明確禁止

forbidden to 禁止

5 confuse [kənˋfjuz] *vt.* 使混亂，混淆

You are just confusing the issue.
你只是讓這個問題更混亂。
dazed and confused 茫然和困惑
confuse the facts 混淆事實

6 weakness [ˋwiknɪs] *n.* 虛弱，軟弱；弱點

What's the cause of his weakness?
他虛弱的原因是什麼？
Can't you see the weakness of his argument?
難道你看不出他爭論的弱點嗎？

7 moderate [ˋmɑdərɪt] *adj.* 溫和的；有節制的

She holds moderate opinions.
她的意見不偏激。
moderate views 溫和的意見

主題 **4**

8 consult [kənˋsʌlt] *vt.* 查閱；與…商量 *vi.* 商議

You had better consult a doctor soon.
你最好快點去看醫生。
consult with 諮詢

9 comply [kəmˋplaɪ] *vi.* 應允，遵照，照做

This business complies with all government regulations.
此業務符合所有政府法規。
You must comply with the teacher's request.
你必須符合老師的要求。

comply with 符合

¹⁰ abide　　[əˋbaɪd]　*vt.*　忍受　*vi.*　持續

Everyone must abide by the law.
所有的人都應遵守法律。
abide by the rules 遵守規則

¹¹ heed　　[hid]　*vi.*　注意到，留心　*n.*　注意

A good leader should always pay heed to the voice of the masses.
一位好領導應該經常注意傾聽群眾的呼聲。
heed your instincts 相信你的直覺
heed the warning 留意警告

¹² grocer　　[ˋgrosɚ]　*n.*　食品商；雜貨商

He's a grocer who owns a small store downtown.
他是在市區擁有一家小商店的雜貨商。
green grocer 蔬菜水果商
grocery store 雜貨店

¹³ useful　　[ˋjusfəl]　*adj.*　有用的；有益的

I think it is a useful book.
我認為這是有用的書。

¹⁴ healthy　　[ˋhɛlθɪ]　*adj.*　健康的

Her innermost thoughts are not healthy.
她心靈深處的思想是不健康的。

15 **gap** [gæp] *n.* 空隙；缺口

We planned to narrow the gap between imports and exports.

我們計畫縮小進出口的差額。

16 **lack** [læk] *n.* 缺縫， *vi.* *vt.* 缺乏，使成缺口

His decision seems to show a lack of political judgment.

他的決定似乎顯示出缺乏政治判斷力。

lack of equality and fairness 缺少平等和不公平

17 **crude** [krud] *adj.* 簡陋的；天然的

China is a country rich in crude oil.

中國是一個原油豐富的國家。

crude drug 天然藥草

18 **fiber** [`faɪbɚ] *n.* 纖維；性格

It was not until 1884 that the first artificial fiber was made.

直到一八八四年，第一個人造纖維才製造出來。

19 **slice** [slaɪs] *n.* 薄片，切片；部分 *vt.* 把…切片；切開 *vi.* 切

I wanted another slice of pizza.

我想要另一片比薩。

20 **foster** [`fɔstɚ] *vt.* 養育，撫養；培養 *adj.* 養育的

The mother tried to foster her son's interest in literature.

母親設法培養兒子對文學的興趣。

foster family 寄養家庭

foster interest in something 培養在一些興趣

21 healthful [ˋhɛlθfəl] *adj.* 有益健康的，使人健康的，衛生的

She leads a healthful life.

她有一個健康的生活。

22 favorable [ˋfevərəb!] *adj.* 有利的；贊成的；討人喜歡的

It is hard to view her conduct in a favorable light.

她的行為實難恭維。

favorable review 良好的評論

favorable conditions 有利條件

23 abound [əˋbaʊnd] *vi.* 充滿，富於

Opportunities abound in the medical field.

機會在醫療領域比比皆是。

24 bounty [ˋbaʊntɪ] *n.* 慷慨，寬大，恩惠

God has given us a great bounty in this new land.

上帝給了我們一個偉大的恩惠在這塊新土地。

25 plentiful [ˋplɛntɪfəl] *adj.* 豐富的，富裕的

The supply of grapes is plentiful this year.

今年葡萄的供應是豐沛的。

plentiful rain 雨量充沛

plentiful harvest 五穀豐收

26 **furnish**　[ˋfɝnɪʃ]　*vt.*　供應，提供；裝備

You are bound to furnish my antagonists with arguments, but not with comprehension.

你一定要向對手提供爭論點，但並無予以理解的必要。

furnish information 提供資料

27 **absorb**　[əbˋsɔrb]　*vt.*　吸收；使專心

Sand absorbs water.

沙吸收水分。

absorb information 吸收資訊

28 **release**　[rɪˋlis]　*vt.*　釋放；放鬆；發表　*n.*　解放；豁免；發行

The army will only release their hostages on certain conditions.

軍隊只有在某些條件下才釋放人質。

主題 4

29 **odour**　[ˈəʊdə(r)]　*n.*　氣味，香氣；味道

The odour summoned up memories of our childhood.

這氣味使我們回憶起孩提時代。

30 **unusual**　[ʌnˋjuʒʊəl]　*adj.*　不常見的；奇異的

She looks on the matter as most unusual.

她認為這件事極不尋常。

Unit
08

Fitness 體適能

Track 44

1 dash [dæʃ] *n.* 猛衝；短跑

He finished first in the 100-meter dash.
他在一百米短跑中得了第一名。

2 difficulty [ˋdɪfəˌkʌltɪ] *adj.* 困難；難事；困境

They experienced great difficulty in getting visas to leave
the country.
他們申請出國簽證經歷了很大的困難。

have some difficulty in getting through 難於接通電話
have some difficulties with pronunciation 在發音方面有困難

3 pant [pænt] *vi.* *vt.* *n.* 喘氣

We began to pant before we reached the top of the
mountain.
我們在到達山頂之前已經在喘氣了。

4 drip [drɪp] *vi.* 滴下；漏水 *n.* 水滴

Sweat is dripping from his forehead.
汗從他額前滴下來。

5 ache [ek] *vi.* 痛；想念 *n.* 疼痛

I ache all over.

我渾身疼痛。

have a headache 頭痛

have aches and pains all over 周身疼痛

6 **stiff** [stɪf] *adj.* 硬的；僵直的

His rather stiff manner puts people off.

他那相當生硬的態度使人們都不敢來。

7 **profitable** [ˈprɑfɪtəbl̩] *adj.* 有利的；有益的

The business is profitable, but just barely.

生意是有盈餘的，只是很少。

8 **extreme** [ɪkˈstrim] *n.* 極端不同的性質

Climbing that mountain was an extreme experience.

攀登那座山是一個極限的經驗。

主題 **4**

9 **youth** [juθ] *n.* 青年

He is an ambitious youth.

他是個野心勃勃的年輕人。

youth hostel 青年招待所

10 **vigour** [ˈvɪgə(r)] *n.* 活力，精力；元氣

He was noted for his vigour.

他以精力充沛而出名。

It takes a lot of vigor to get through medical school.

熬過醫學院需要很多精力。

11 **hale** [hel] *adj.* 強壯的，健壯的

Grandfather will be 85 years old, but he is hale and hearty.

祖父就要 85 歲高齡了，但仍精神矍鑠。

12 **hardy** [`hɑrdɪ] *adj.* 強壯的，耐勞的

He is a hardy soul. Being sick won't slow him down.

他是一個勇敢的人。生病並沒有讓他慢下來。

winter-hardy 耐寒的

hardy perennial 多年生耐寒植物

13 **remarkable** [rɪ`mɑrkəbl] *adj.* 異常的，非凡的

The boy has a remarkable talent.

男孩有著非凡的天賦。

【同】bizarre, outlandish

【反】inconspious

14 **specimen** [`spɛsəmən] *n.* 樣本，標本，樣品

He is still a fine specimen of health.

他仍是健康的典範。

【同】sample, instance, example

15 **ability** [ə`bɪlətɪ] *n.* 能力；能耐，本領

She has shown some ability with language.

她已經表現出一些語言的能力。

16 **devote** [dɪˋvot] *vt.* 將⋯奉獻，致力於

I've devoted a lot of my free time to my son's soccer team.
我投入很多我的自由時間給兒子的足球隊。

devote all one's life to doing sth. 某人的整個一生都致力於做某事
devote hours to standing there 幾個小時都站在那裡

17 **gym** [dʒɪm] *n.* （口語）體育館，健身房

They play badminton in the nearest gym every Saturday.
每個星期六他們都去最近的體育館打羽毛球。

18 **diligence** [ˋdɪlədʒəns] *n.* 勤奮

He has shown a great amount of diligence in finishing the project.
在完成的專案中，他表現得很勤奮。

to amend stupidity by diligence 以勤補拙

19 **accustom** [əˋkʌstəm] *vt.* 使習慣

We accustomed ourselves to the new house slowly.
我們慢慢地習慣了自己的新家。

20 **excess** [ɪkˋsɛs] *n.* 超越；過量；過度

The fat man went on a diet to get rid of his excess weight.
這個胖男人節制飲食以減輕過量的體重。

excess baggage 超重行李
excess load 超負載

主題 4

21 **achieve**　[əˋtʃiv]　*vt.*　完成，實現；達到

They managed to achieve a kind of modus vivendi.
他們設法達成了某種臨時的妥協。
achieve the first price 獲得一等獎
achieve experience 獲得經驗

22 **elevate**　[ˋɛlə͵vet]　*vt.*　提高（思想）；抬高

Reading good books elevates your mind.
閱讀好書使人思想高尚。
They elevated him to the role of president.
他們提升他的主席的角色。

23 **perpetual**　[pɚˋpɛtʃʊəl]　*adj.*　永久的；四季開花的

He has a perpetual income from his grandfather's estate.
從他的祖父遺產中，他有永久的收入。
perpetual calendar 萬年曆
perpetual insurance 終生保險

24 **intend**　[ɪnˋtɛnd]　*vt.*　想要，打算；意指

My sister intended to catch the early train, but she didn't get up in time.
我妹妹本來打算趕早班的火車，但是她起晚了。
【同】plan, mean, propose

25 **triumph**　[ˋtraɪəmf]　*n.*　凱旋；勝利　*vi.*　成功

They triumph over their rivals.
他們戰勝了他們的競爭對手。

26 remain   [rɪˋmen]   *vi.*   保持，仍是；剩下

She remained poor all her life.

她終生貧窮。

remaining cigarettes 剩餘的煙頭

remain the same as before 保持像以前一樣

27 champion   [ˋtʃæmpɪən]   *n.*   鬥士；提倡者

The champion is in training for his next fight.

這位冠軍為了下一場比賽正在進行訓練。

28 lavish   [ˋlævɪʃ]   *adj.*   浪費的；過度的

This is a vast and lavish party.

這是個規模盛大、極其鋪張的宴會。

lavish on 大肆揮霍

【同】generous

【反】thrifty, economical

29 stature   [ˋstætʃɚ]   *n.*   身高，身材；評價

His achievements have given him high stature among his colleagues.

因為他的成就，同事之間給了他超高的評價。

30 immortal   [ɪˋmɔrtl̩]   *adj.*   不朽的；永生的

She left behind an immortal example to all posterity.

她給後世留下了不朽的典範。

主題 **4**

Medication 藥物

Track 45

1 **injurious** [ɪnˋdʒʊrɪəs] *adj.* 有害的

Smoking is injurious to your health.

吸煙對健康有害。

【同】harmful, poisonous

【反】beneficial, useful

2 **abuse** [əˋbjus] *vt.* 濫用；虐待 *n.* 濫用

He abuses his body when he smokes.

當他抽煙時，他在虐待自己的身體。

3 **organ** [ˋɔrgən] *n.* 器官；機構；管風琴

The heart is one of the body's vital organs.

心臟是人體的重要器官之一。

4 **neglect** [nɪgˋlɛkt] *vt.* 忽視，忽略；疏忽

The last thing that he'll neglect is his children's education.

他不可能忽視他小孩的教育。

5 **fearful** [ˋfɪrfəl] *adj.* 害怕的，可怕的

There is a fearful explosion.

有可怕的爆炸聲。

6 dread   [drɛd]   *n.*   畏懼；恐怖   *vt.*   懼怕

He dreads Mondays, as he has to go back to work.
他很怕星期一，因為要去上班。

He dreaded seeing his mother after getting arrested.
他被捕後害怕看到他的母親。

7 anxious   [ˋæŋkʃəs]   *adj.*   渴望的；憂慮的

We are anxious for the men who are out on the boat.
我們擔心著在船上的男人。

be anxious about sb. 為某人擔心（擔憂）

be anxious to leave 急於離開

8 refrain   [rɪˋfren]   *vi.*   抑制，制止，忍住

Please refrain from talking during the presentation.
請不要在演講中交談。

refrain from 忍住，制止

9 abstain   [əbˋsten]   *v.*   自動戒絕，抑制

My dad swore to abstain from smoking.
我爸爸發誓要戒煙。

【反】indulge

10 avail   [əˋvel]   *vt.*   有益於   *n.*   效用

The medicine is of no avail.
這藥無效。

【同】contribute, benefit

主題 **4**

11 **physician**　[fɪ`zɪʃən]　*n.*　醫生，內科醫生

The physician splits his time between the hospital and the clinic.

醫生把醫院和診所之間時間劃分開來。

That physician has a good bedside manner.

該醫生有一個良好的巡房態度。

12 **prescribe**　[prɪ`skraɪb]　*vt.*　命令；處（方）

The doctor will prescribe medication for your condition.

醫生將為您的病情開藥。

13 **unit**　[`junɪt]　*n.*　單位；單元；部件

This textbook has thirty units.

這本課本有三十單元。

in this unit 在這個單元裡

unit two 第二單元

14 **dose**　[dos]　*n.*　劑量，用量；一劑

Give him a dose of his own medicine.

【諺】以其人之道還治其人之身。

【同】dosage, portion

15 **tablet**　[`tæblɪt]　*n.*　碑，匾；藥片

Please fill a glass with water and dissolve this tablet in it.

倒杯水把藥片放進去溶解了。

【同】pill

16 balm　　[bɑm]　*n.*　香油，藥膏

He smeared some balm on his hand to soothe the pain.

他在手上塗了些藥膏來止痛。

17 constitute　　[ˋkɑnstə,tjut]　*vt.*　構成，組成

Young people constitute a large part of the unemployed.

年輕人在失業者中佔了很大一部分。

【同】compose, comprise, form

18 contain　　[kənˋten]　*vt.*　包含，容納；等於

The atlas contains twenty maps.

這個地圖集有二十幅地圖。

feel the box containing sth. 摸裝著某東西的盒子

find sth. containing 32,000 Chinese metal coins 發現某個包含
32000 個中國的金屬幣的東西

19 dispense　　[dɪˋspɛns]　*vt.*　分配

The teacher dispenses equal justice to all students.

老師對所有學生一律公平對待。

主題 **4**

20 complaint　　[kəmˋplent]　*n.*　疾病，病痛；主訴

We made a complaint about our noisy neighbors.

我們對我們吵鬧的鄰居提出投訴。

file a complaint 控告

complaint department 客訴部門

21 odor　[`odə]　*n.*　氣味

The odor from the farm was unpleasant.

農場的氣味令人不舒服。

odorant 有氣味的東西

22 drowsy　[`draʊzɪ]　*adj.*　昏昏欲睡的

The medicine made me drowsy, so I didn't want to drive.

藥讓我昏昏欲睡，所以我不想開車。

drowsy away 昏昏沉沉地消磨

drowse off 打瞌睡

23 dreary　[`drɪərɪ]　*adj.*　沉悶的，乏味的

The weather there is dreary and depressing in the winter.

在那裡冬天的天氣是沉悶和沮喪的。

【同】gloomy, dull, dark

24 continue　[kən`tɪnjʊ]　*vt.*　繼續，連續；延伸

We continued to study well past midnight.

我們繼續研究到過了午夜。

continue to do sth. 繼續做某事

continue with 繼續做

25 remedy　[`rɛmədɪ]　*n.　vt.*　治療；補救

The remedy is to eat less and exercise more.

治療方式是少吃多運動。

26 **suppress**　　[səˋprɛs]　*vt.*　　鎮壓；抑制；隱瞞

The government had suppressed the truth for more than twenty years.

政府已經隱瞞那事實超過 20 年。

【同】crush, quell, repress, squash

【反】express

27 **relieve**　　[rɪˋliv]　*vt.*　　減輕，解除；救濟

This medicine will relieve your headache.

這藥將減輕你的頭痛。

28 **heal**　　[hil]　*vt.*　　治癒；使和解

The cut will heal itself in a couple days.

傷口將在幾天癒合。

29 **conquer**　　[ˏkɑŋkɚ]　*vt.*　　征服

When will scientists conquer cancer?

科學家什麼時候才能征服癌症呢？

主題 4

30 **jocund**　　[ˋdʒɑkənd]　*adj.*　　快樂的，高興的

I cannot be gay in such a jocund company.

我和如此快樂的同伴在一起豈能不樂。

Unit 10

Illness 疾病

Track 46

1 infirmity [ɪnˈfɝˌmɪtɪ] *n.* 虛弱

That injury has caused a temporary infirmity.
這傷害已經造成暫時的虛弱。

2 amiss [əˈmɪs] *adj.* 有毛病的，出差錯的

A word of compliment may not come amiss.
讚美並無壞處。

amiss in 不對勁的

【同】awry

3 sickness [ˈsɪknɪs] *n.* 疾病

The doctor healed them of their sickness.
那位醫生治好了他們的疾病。

4 injury [ˈɪndʒərɪ] *n.* 損害，傷害；受傷處

Most people protect themselves from injury to their self-esteem.
大多數人保護自己使自尊心不受傷害。

inflict an injury upon 造成傷害

add insult to injury 雪上加霜

【同】insult, harm, damage, wound

5 **treatment** [`tritmənt] *n.* 待遇；治療，療法

He should follow his treatment with plenty of rest in bed.

他應該在治療之後好好臥床休息。

6 **aggravate** [`ægrə,vet] *v.* 加重，惡化

Ice water aggravated my toothache.

冰水使我的牙痛加重了。

【同】intensify, remedy

【反】lessen

7 **induce** [ɪn`djus] *vt.* 勸誘；引起；感應

We had to induce labor because the baby was late.

因為寶寶超過預產期，我們必須引產。

【同】coax, tempt

8 **flu** [flu] *n.* 流行性感冒

He's been in bed for two days with the flu.

他因為流感一直在床上躺了兩天。

主題 **4**

9 **fever** [`fivɚ] *n.* 發熱，發燒；狂熱

The baby has a slight fever.

小嬰兒有點發燒。

have a high (slight) fever 發高燒（有點燒）

suffer fever 發燒

10 **thermometer** [θɚˋmɑmətɚ] *n.* 溫度計，體溫計

The thermometer registered 30 degrees.

溫度計顯示的讀數為 30 度。

11 **examination** [ɪɡˏzæməˋneʃən] *n.* 檢查；考試

The doctor gave him an examination to see if he had chest trouble.

醫生給他做了檢查，看他是否有肺病。

12 **shock** [ʃɑk] *n.* 衝擊；震驚 *vi.* 震動

Her death was a great shock to us all.

她的死使我們大家都大為震驚。

13 **unexpected** [ˏʌnɪkˋspɛktɪd] *adj.* 想不到的，意外的

Mr. Green paid me an unexpected visit.

格林先生出乎意料地前來看我。

【同】unforeseen, unanticipated

【反】consequent, usual

14 **linger** [ˋlɪŋgɚ] *vi.* 逗留，徘徊；拖延

He lingered outside the school after everybody else had gone home.

別人回家後，他仍在學校外面徘徊。

【同】haunt

【反】hasten

15 sickly   [`sıklı]   *adj.*   病弱的，陰沉的，無精打采的

She was a week, sickly child.

她是一個體弱多病的孩子。

16 wan   [wɑn]   *adj.*   虛弱的，病態的

She gave a wan smile and said she was all right.

她給了一個虛弱的微笑，說她很好。

【同】ashen, ghastly, lunar

17 sullen   [`sʌlın]   *adj.*   繃著臉不高興的

He was a sullen man, with a quick temper.

他是一個鬱鬱寡歡、脾氣暴躁的人。

sullen mood 憂鬱的心情

【同】moody, gloomy, dark

【反】cheerful

18 agony   [`ægənı]   *n.*   極度痛苦

The defeat left him in agony.

失敗讓他極度痛苦。

19 throughout   [θru`aʊt]   *prep.*   遍及

It snowed throughout the night.

雪整整下了一夜。

throughout the world 全世界

throughout one's whole life 某人的整個一生

主題 4

20 liver　[ˋlɪvɚ]　*n.*　肝；肝臟

He's got cancer in his liver.

他得了肝癌。

21 cancer　[ˋkænsɚ]　*n.*　癌，癌症，腫瘤

He was afflicted with cancer.

他患了癌症。

22 fatal　[ˋfetl]　*adj.*　致命的；命運的

Failure is not fatal. Keep moving on.

失敗並非末日。繼續前進吧。

fatal flaw 致命的缺陷

fatalism　*n.*　宿命論

23 invalid　[ˋɪnvəlɪd]　*n.*　病人　*adj.*　有病的

The nurse took care of the invalid carefully.

護士細心地照顧這個病人。

【同】null, useless, void

【反】strong

24 tragedy　[ˋtrædʒədɪ]　*n.*　悲劇；慘事，慘案

The tragedy was all over.

悲劇結束了。

【同】adversity, misfortune

【反】comedy

25 perish　[ˋpɛrɪʃ]　*vi.*　死亡，夭折；枯萎

Hundreds of people perished in the earthquake.

數百人死於那次地震。

26 decease [dɪˋsis] *n.* 死亡

His decease made us very sad.

他的去世使我們非常悲傷。

27 grieve [griv] *vt.* 使悲痛 *vi.* 悲痛

She was grieving for the dead dog.

她為死去的狗悲傷。

28 sympathy [ˋsɪmpəθɪ] *n.* 同情；同感；慰問

The sad story stirred his sympathy.

這傷心的故事激起了他的同情心。

show sympathy for 對…表同情

in sympathy with 同情

29 revive [rɪˋvaɪv] *vt.* *vi.* 甦醒；復興

Her kiss revived the fallen prince.

她的親吻讓倒下的王子甦醒。

【同】resuscitate, reanimate

30 miracle [ˋmɪrək!] *n.* 奇蹟

It's a miracle that he defeated the cancer.

他抗癌成功是個奇蹟。

sacred miracle 神聖的奇蹟

miracle drug 特效藥

主題 4

Unit 11

Skin Care 護膚

Track 47

1 **wrinkle** [`rɪŋk!] *n.* 皺紋 *vt.* 使起皺紋 *vi.* 皺起來

His clothes were wrinkled.

他的衣服皺皺的。

2 **chap** [tʃæp] *n.* 龜裂 *vt.* （皮膚）變粗糙，龜裂 *vi.* 出現龜裂

The wind made my lips very chapped.

風把我的嘴唇吹得非常乾。

This medicine will relieve chapped skin.

這種藥能緩解皮膚龜裂。

chap stick 護唇膏

3 **mix** [mɪks] *vt.* 使混合；使攪和 *vi.* 相混合；交往

You can't mix oil with water.

你不能把油和水混合。

a mixed group 男女生混合小組

mix together 混合到一起

4 **moisture** [`mɔɪstʃɚ] *n.* 潮濕，濕氣；溫度

Lotion will add moisture to your skin.

乳液將會保濕你的皮膚。

moisture content 水分含量

5　**jar**　[dʒɑr]　*n.*　罎子；罐子；缸

The pickles were in a big jar.

泡菜在一個大罐子裡。

a jar of jam 一瓶果醬

wine jars 酒瓶

6　**squeeze**　[skwiz]　*vt.*　*vi.*　榨，擠；壓榨

You can squeeze those oranges and get some delicious juice.

你可以擠壓這些橘子並得到一些美味果汁。

squeeze between 擠壓之間

squeeze out 榨出，擠出

7　**fluid**　[ˋfluɪd]　*n.*　流體，液體　*adj.*　不固定的

Air is a fluid but not a liquid, while water is both a fluid and a liquid.

空氣是流體不是液體，水是流體也是液體。

fluid ounce 液量單位

8　**liquid**　[ˋlɪkwɪd]　*n.*　液體　*adj.*　液體的

Plasma is a clear yellow liquid.

血漿是種透明淡黃的液體。

liquid air 液態空氣

liquid capital 流動資本

9 **apply** [əˋplaɪ] *vt.* 塗；應用，實施，使用 *vi.* 申請

I applied for that job last week.

我上週申請了這項工作。

You have to apply what you learned to solve the problems.

你需要應用你學到的來解決問題。

10 **anoint** [əˋnɔɪnt] *vt.* 塗以油或軟膏，施以塗油

The priest anoints the baby's forehead.

牧師在嬰兒的前額上施塗油。

11 **surface** [ˋsɝfɪs] *n.* 地面，表面；外表 *adj.* 地面上的
vt. 使……浮出水面 *vi.* 呈現

The surface of the moon is not smooth.

月球的表面是不光滑的。

12 **forehead** [ˋfɔr,hɛd] *n.* 額頭，前部

My mother passed her hand across her forehead.

我媽媽用手抹了一下額頭。

13 **often** [ˋɔfən] *adv.* 經常，常常

How often do you go there?

你多長時間去一次那裡？

14 **restraint** [rɪˋstrent] *n.* 抑制；遏制；克制

Seat belts are effective restraints.

安全帶是有效的約束。

safety restraint 安全約束

restraint of trade 貿易管制

15 rarely [ˋrɛrlɪ] *adv.* 很少，難得

I rarely have drinks.

我很少喝酒。

16 glow [glo] *n.* 白熱光　*vi.* 發白熱光

That kind of paint glows in the dark.

這種塗料在黑暗中發光。

glowworm 螢火蟲

17 lighten [ˋlaɪtn] *vt.* 照亮，使明亮　*vi.* 變亮

Asian women often try to lighten their skin.

亞洲女性常常試圖美白他們的皮膚。

lighten out 閃現出

18 neat [nit] *adj.* 整潔的；整齊的

The headmaster praised the students for their neat turn-out.

校長表揚學生服裝整齊。

19 image [ˋɪmɪdʒ] *n.* 像；形象　*vt.* 想像

This company is concerned about its corporate image.

這家公司關心它企業形象。

20 distinction [dɪˋstɪŋkʃən] *n.* 差別，不同，區分

You have the distinction of being the first person done.

你必須做到和別人區分開來。

主題 4

21 **attraction** [ə`trækʃən] *n.* 吸引；吸引力；引力

She felt a strong attraction to him.

她感到他對她有強烈的吸引力。

magnetic attraction 磁吸引力

attractive quality 魅力品質

22 **flattery** [`flætərɪ] *n.* 諂媚，阿諛，巴結

Flattery is a sure way to a girl's heart.

奉承是一種方法贏得女孩的心。

insincere flattery 缺乏誠意的阿諛

flatter myself 自我吹捧

23 **bewitch** [bɪ`wɪtʃ] *vt.* 施魔法於，迷惑，使著迷

The witch bewitched the prince and turned him into a fat pig.

女巫對王子施魔法，將他變成一隻肥豬。

24 **resist** [rɪ`zɪst] *vt. vi.* 抵抗；抵制 *n.* 抗蝕劑

They couldn't resist his plea for help.

他們無法拒絕他的懇求幫忙。

25 **comparative** [kəm`pærətɪv] *adj.* 比較的，相對的 *n.* 【語】比較級

A hippocampus's brain is comparatively small.

河馬的大腦是比較小的。

comparative literature 比較文學

26 pretty [`prɪtɪ] *adj.* 漂亮的，標緻的　*adv.* 相當　*n.* 漂亮的人　*vt.* 使漂亮

He has a pretty daughter.
他有個可愛的女兒。

It's pretty cold today.
今天相當冷。

27 astonishment [ə`stɑnɪʃmənt] *n.* 驚奇，驚訝

They all stared in astonishment.
他們全都驚訝地瞪著眼。

28 reverence [`rɛvərəns] *n.* 崇敬，敬禮　*vt.* 尊敬

You must show reverence when you are in the temple.
當在寺廟時你必須表現崇敬。

reverence for God 對上帝的愛和尊敬

29 adore [ə`dor] *vt.* 崇拜；很喜歡

He adores the teddy bear he got when he was a baby.
當他是小嬰兒時，他最喜歡泰迪熊了。

30 embrace [ɪm`bres] *n.* 懷抱　*vt.* 包括，包含；包圍　*vi.* 擁抱

My mom embraces me in a hug when I get home.
當我回家時，媽媽給我一個擁抱。

embrace an idea 接受一個想法

主題 4

Mental 心理

 Track 48

1 frailty [ˋfreltɪ] *n.* 脆弱，弱點

One of the frailties of human nature is greediness.

人性的弱點之一是貪婪。

human frailty 人性的弱點

2 suffer [ˋsʌfɚ] *vi.* 受苦 *vt.* 遭受

She couldn't suffer criticism.

她受不了批評。

suffer a lot of pain 受了很多痛苦

suffer from a strange illness 得了一種怪病

3 inner [ˋɪnɚ] *adj.* 內部的；內心的

She has no inner resources and hates to be alone.

她沒有內在的精神寄託，因而害怕孤獨。

inner voice 內心的聲音

4 emotion [ɪˋmoʃən] *n.* 感情；情緒；激動

She choked with emotion.

她激動得說不出話來。

feel great emotion 感受滿懷深情

emotional appeal 情緒感染

5 feeling   [`filɪŋ]   *n.*   感情；感覺，知覺   *adj.*   動人的

He lost all feeling in his toes.

他的腳趾完全失去了知覺。

hurt one's feelings 傷了某人的感情

6 frail   [frel]   *adj.*   脆弱的；意志薄弱的

She was always a frail girl and easily hurt.

她總是意志薄弱的且易受傷害的女孩。

7 dismal   [`dɪzm!]   *adj.*   陰沉的，憂鬱的

The rain and wind made for a dismal day on the golf course.

風雨使高爾夫球課的天氣陰沉。

took a dismal view of the economy.

對經濟抱著不樂觀的看法

dismal science 政治經濟學

主題 4

8 melancholy   [`mɛlən,kɑlɪ]   *n.*   *adj.*   憂鬱（的），悲傷

There is a vein of melancholy in his character.

他的性格中有少許憂鬱的氣質。

feel melancholy 感到憂鬱

melancholic 憂鬱症患者

9 gloom   [glum]   *n.*   黑暗；憂愁   *vi.*   變陰暗   *vt.*   使憂鬱

The gloom he usually felt was not present when he awoke.

當他醒來時，他通常有的憂鬱不在了。

10 anguish [ˋæŋgwɪʃ] *n.* 極大痛苦　*vt.* 使極度痛苦
vi. 感到萬分痛苦

They anguished over whether to move for a long time.
有很長的時間他們對於不確定是否搬家感到萬分痛苦。

11 dismay [dɪsˋme] *n.* 驚慌，沮喪，灰心　*vt.* 使驚慌
Lucy's face registered dismay.
露西臉上流露出驚慌的神色

12 torment [tɔrˋmɛnt] *n.* 痛苦　*vt.* 折磨
His memories of battle tormented him at night.
他戰鬥的回憶在晚上折磨著他。

13 despair [dɪˋspɛr] *n.* 絕望；失望　*vi.* 喪失信心
That was the result of despair, as he didn't know what else to do.
這是絕望的結果，因為他不知道自己還能做些什麼。

14 temper [ˋtɛmpɚ] *n.* 韌度；心情，情緒　*vt.* 鍛鍊
vi. （金屬）經回火後的韌度

She slammed the door in a temper.
她生氣地摔門。

temper justice with mercy 恩威並濟

15 **stormy**　　[`stɔrmɪ]　　*adj.*　　有暴風雨的；激烈的

The couple had a stormy quarrel.

這對夫妻激烈爭吵。

stormy weather 暴風雨天氣

stormy temper 暴風雨的般脾氣

16 **furious**　　[`fjʊərɪəs]　　*adj.*　　狂暴的；強烈的

He was furious at his son when the police came.

當員警來到時，他對他的兒子感到非常憤怒。

to be furious to fly into 大發雷霆

17 **guilt**　　[gɪlt]　　*n.*　　有罪，犯罪；內疚

His best friend corroborated his guilt.

他最好的朋友證實了他的犯罪。

guilty conscience 內疚

guilty party 有罪一方

18 **misery**　　[`mɪzərɪ]　　*n.*　　痛苦，悲慘，不幸

His misery will not end soon.

他的痛苦不會很快結束。

misery loves company 同病相憐

19 **temperate**　　[`tɛmprɪt]　　*adj.*　　有節制的；溫和的

The climate here is quite temperate.

這裡的氣候比較溫和。

temperate zone 溫帶

temperate climate 溫帶氣候

20 **happily** [ˈhæpɪlɪ] *adv.* 幸福地，快樂地，幸好

He reacted happily to the good news.
他愉快地回應了好消息。
happy medium 中庸之道

21 **mature** [məˈtjʊr] *vt.* 使成熟 *vi.* 成熟 *adj.* 穩重的

He doesn't act very mature for his age.
以他的年齡，他沒有採取很成熟的行動。
mature soil 成熟土壤
mature student 成人學生

22 **redeem** [rɪˈdim] *v.* 贖罪，實踐（諾言）

You can redeem this coupon for a free drink.
此券可以兌換免費飲料。
redeemable 可贖回的
redeeming feature 可取之處

23 **yourself** [jʊɚˈsɛlf] *pron.* 你自己；你親自

Just be yourself; they can't take that away from you.
只是你自己；他們無法改變你。
by yourself 靠自己

24 **solve** [sɑlv] *vt.* 解答；解決 *vi.* 作解答

I think I can solve the problem.
我想我能解決這問題。
solvent extraction 溶劑萃取

25 repose [rɪ`poz] *n.* 歇息 *vi.* 躺著休息，安睡 *vt.* 使休息

She reposed on a lounge chair.
她在躺椅上休息。

26 assure [ə`ʃʊr] *vt.* 使確信；向…保證

I can assure you that your kids will be happy here.
我可以向你保證，你小孩在這裡會很快樂的。

27 excellent [`ɛkslənt] *adj.* 極好的，優秀的

This hall would make an excellent theatre.
這座大廳可當作極好的劇院。

28 grin [grɪn] *n.* 露齒的笑 *vi.* 咧著嘴笑 *vt.* 露齒笑著表示

The boys grinned with pleasure when I gave them the candies.
當我給男孩們糖果時，他們高興地咧開嘴笑了。

grin and bear it 逆來順受

主題 4

29 mirth [mɝθ] *n.* 歡樂，歡笑

He is a pleasant person, full of mirth.
他是一個開朗的人充滿歡笑。

30 bliss [blɪs] *n.* 福佑，天賜的福

He had a blissful feeling on his wedding day.
在他的婚禮上，他有一種幸福的感覺。

bliss out 欣喜若狂

Leader 035

開啟生活主題字彙聯想力(MP3)

作　　　者	力得編輯群
發 行 人	周瑞德
執行總監	齊心瑀
執行編輯	魏于婷
校　　　對	編輯部
封面構成	高鍾琪

內頁構成	華漢電腦排版有限公司
印　　　製	大亞彩色印刷製版股份有限公司
初　　　版	2016 年 1 月
定　　　價	新台幣 349 元
出　　　版	力得文化
電　　　話	(02) 2351-2007
傳　　　真	(02) 2351-0887
地　　　址	100 台北市中正區福州街 1 號 10 樓之 2
E - m a i l	best.books.service@gmail.com
網　　　址	www.bestbookstw.com

港澳地區總經銷	泛華發行代理有限公司
地　　　址	香港新界將軍澳工業邨駿昌街 7 號 2 樓
電　　　話	(852) 2798-2323
傳　　　真	(852) 2796-5471

國家圖書館出版品預行編目資料

開啟生活主題字彙聯想力 / 力得編輯群著. -- 初版. --
臺北市 : 力得文化, 2016.01
　面 ；　公分. -- (Leader ; 35)
ISBN 978-986-92398-4-4(平裝附光碟片)

1.英語 2.詞彙

　　805.12　　　104027784